THE

SOCIALISTS

OF SHOE CITY

The Socialist Movement In

Haverhill, Massachusetts

Copyright @2024

Preface

As a lifelong resident of Haverhill deeply connected to its rich history, I've been captivated by its legacy of socialism and its enduring impact on our community. My journey exploring Haverhill's socialist movement began during my tenure as a social studies teacher at Haverhill High School, where I taught the city's history for several years. It was then that I stumbled upon the remarkable story of Haverhill's socialist mayor in an old trivia book by fellow educator Pat Garwich.

Teaching allowed me to delve deeper into Haverhill's socialist era, revealing the profound influence of socialist ideals on the city's development. This exploration became personal as many of my family members, including my grandmother Elmina Pitocchelli, worked in the shoe factories that once dominated Haverhill. Erminia, who immigrated from Italy in the late 19th century, shared stories of her experiences in the local shoe industry, instilling in me a belief in community and social progress.

Inspired by my grandmother's legacy and my experiences as an educator and activist, I embarked on a journey to chronicle the history of socialism in Haverhill. "The Socialists of Shoe City: The Socialist Movement in Haverhill, Massachusetts" is the result of years of research and a deep commitment to preserving the legacy of those who fought for social and economic justice in our community.

The connection to the shoe industry runs deep in my family's history. Erminia's brother, Arthur Altieri, worked as a foreman in several shoe shops, even running his own small shop in California later in life. Other family members, like Donnie Campana and Julie Kellam, also had ties to the industry. My mother, Evelyn Brown, briefly worked in a Plaistow factory before pursuing a career in beauty, eventually owning Evelyn's Beauty Salon in downtown Haverhill for over 50 years.

The prevalence of shoe industry jobs in our family's history reflects the broader impact of this industry on Haverhill's economy. Even Erminia's father, once a cobbler in Italy, had a small shop where he performed various tasks related to shoe repair and tailoring.

What exactly constitutes socialism?

The term "socialism" carries diverse interpretations, even among self-proclaimed socialists. Textbook definitions outline its key features:

Capitalism entails private ownership of production means, market competition, and profit motives, with goods and services distributed via market supply and demand. In contrast, socialism involves communal or state ownership and control of production means, aiming for social and economic equality. Communism advocates collective ownership, envisioning a classless society where resources are allocated based on need, often through a stateless, moneyless system.

Various socialist schools of thought, such as Marxism, Democratic Socialism, Libertarian Socialism, Anarcho-Syndicalism, and Utopian Socialism, offer distinct approaches to achieving socialist goals. In this book, you'll discover Haverhill socialists' unique perspectives on implementing socialism in local governance.

I've hesitated to write this book for years due to concerns about perceived political bias. While I have the right to advocate, my focus lies on highlighting this era's significance in American history and politics. Additionally, I've questioned my ability to do justice to this story. However, as historian David McCollough once said, "If you get one good idea from a book, it was a good read." I'm confident readers will find valuable insights within these pages.

Table of Contents

CHAPTER 1

Introduction to Haverhill Socialism

This is the story of 20th-century socialism in Massachusetts as grassroots activism, uniting working classes, and bringing about transforming political change. Tucked into the industrial setting of Haverhill, this place became the unlikely cocoon for the fiery red psychiatrist, where visionaries and passionate leaders uncompromisingly combated the status quo and defied tradition in the fight for a more human, kinder society in which each person would be valued and cherished.

Socialism in Haverhill was germinated by the intolerable working conditions, labor action by the workers, and the visionary ideals prevalent in society at the turn of the last century. The lack of creature comforts for factory workers and the miserable backbreaking hours that followed hard and fast in the extended, unrelenting industrialization—low wages, long hours, and deplorable working conditions—brought a radical evaluation of the social contract. Individuals, among them immigrants and members of the underserved classes that had flocked to Haverhill for their seemingly better future, found themselves under the command of large factory owners and a system of production focused on maximization of profits for the latter.

In capitalism that distorted the essence of community and relationships, in this hostile environment, a group of few people who were daring to think differently about things started dissenting against capitalism's fundamental assumptions. They wanted to replace the capitalistic society with a different kind of society; it is their dream society, where cooperation, equality, and collective ownership of the means of production are the ideals. They were quite open-minded and inspired by intellectual socialists like Karl Marx and Frederick Engels. Their socialism was the weapon to fight the exploitation of workers and secure a fair share of the labor fruits for everyone.

Among the socialist warriors who set out on the socialist path were one young intellectual, James F. Carey, and another, Albert L. Couch, who were the big names in the Haverhill history of socialism. The shoe worker, as well as a union leader turned political organizer, indeed had a smart mind and a good shot at oratory that made him the best speaker of the Carey King class. Couch was disenchanted with the existing religious lack of idealism and indifference but had a zeal for socialism, where he thought he could demonstrate the ultimate expression of serving humanity.

Carey and Couch became the foundation of Haverhill's initial phase of socialism, never resting in their persistent calls for workers' rights, economic autonomy, and the fairness of society. They formally constituted the Haverhill Socialist Labor Party in 1895, and that became a hub for learning as well as activism and organizing. The way that SLPs gave public lectures, organized study groups, and held agitated discussions was a catalyst for the transformation of socialist thought during that time when the local workers were used to conventional wisdom.

Consequently, as the SLP became more and more powerful and came to have a bigger and bigger impact on the socialist movement in Haverhill, socialism became more and more prominent. At the very heart of the city, people from unions and social places were starting to wake up to the power that the masses possess and how they can use it to change the status quo. They were active as members of cooperatives and mutual aid societies in accumulating wealth and assisting each other during difficult periods. They conducted strikes and boycotts to convince employers to offer better pay and working conditions in the face of intimidation and violence from their employers and their private security details. They gradually realized that the struggle for existence was no longer a fight that they had to carry out alone but a huge, gigantic movement that deepened their social and economic freedoms.

Nevertheless, the elevation of Haverhill to socialism came with its problems and struggles. Official leaders of political and economic establishments viewed growing democratic supporters as enemies of the city. The authorities, as well as the factory owners and their government allies, did not hold back from using any means of suppression, deploying red-baiting propaganda and blunt repression. Socialist freedom fighters constantly faced threats of torture, incarceration, and even beatings for simply standing up against capitalist repression.

However, despite these challenges, the social movement in Haverhill proceeded to expand and develop further and further In 1898, in a most unexpected election, James F. Carey was elected as an SLP member of the Massachusetts State Legislature instead of being the first president. His victory resonated through the entire political structure and further incited socialists of many classes to put in extra effort.

The resolute pursuit of progressive policies and an unwavering champion of the working class were the legacy of Carey's time as an elected official. He proposed measures such as the limitation of child labor, the introduction of a minimum wage, and public ownership of utilities—revolutionary concepts at that time that turned into the fundamental parts of the progressive agenda in later times. Even though his projects were beaten by the machine of the old state political system, Carey always stood for the shift in dialogue terms and laid the foundation for future victories.

In Haverhill, the socialist movement kept moving and changing considering the new situations. In 1900, a group of socialists, led by Albert Couch and several other S.L.P. members, formed a new organization known as the Social Democratic Party (S.D.P.), later renamed the Socialist Party of America. The SDP, on the other hand, took a more moderate and election-oriented approach to socialism, focusing on gradual reform as opposed to revolutionary change. Some embraced this development as a broader acceptance and pragmatic step, while others viewed it as a betrayal of socialist principles and a submission to the system they wanted to change.

Even with that internal tension, the socialist movement in Haverhill was still very powerful and continued to make changes. In the years to come, socialists had a leading hand in many of the city's substantial labor fights, from the 1902 Luster Union strike to the 'Bread and Roses' strike of 1912 that involved textile workers. They never gave up the struggle for political reform, which they pursued by running for local and state office and also establishing partnerships with progressive forces in society. They still played an important role in the city's intellectual and cultural life, organizing talks, concerts, and other events to unite the citizens of diverse groups who had a common purpose and sense of solidarity.

As the twentieth century swept the nation, the social movement in Haverhill would encounter brand new challenges and chances. The First World War and the Russian Revolution brought about such profound changes in the political map of the world that socialists had to take another look at their existing strategies and affiliations everywhere. Fascism's rise and the Great Depression would be extreme tests of socialist theory and call into question many of the movement's aims, while the New Deal and post-war welfare state would absorb and fulfill many of the socialists' major demands. But the spirit of socialism in

Haverhill will continue to live in new generations of activists and reformers who will go on to stand up for a more just and humane world.

We live today facing the crises that our time has brought—rampant inequality, environmental degradation, and eroding democracy. In this context, the story of Haverhill's socialism gains relevance and urgency. From those settlers of old, we learned to draw lessons and power. Their example made us understand that ordinary people possess the ability to influence even the most spectacular changes. Through their pursuit, we can acquire meaningful teachings about the significance of solidarity, the untenability of disorganization, and the energizing nature of socialist ideologies.

The history of Haverhill socialism is not quite a straightforward moral tale or a guide for how we can act today. Being a typical human worldly venture, it was characterized by inconsistencies, faults, and unintentional outcomes. The movement could not be exempt from the prejudices and defects of a bygone era, and its actions did not always match its principles. which constituted its highest ideal. Its leaders were fallible people, and this was full of partial and incomplete successes, though.

And so, Haverhill socialism's ultimate victory or failure isn't what matters, but instead the example of what can be done if we join forces in striving for a shared vision. In fact, of unbeatable preference, of great revolution and destruction, the socialists of Haverhill dream about a better world, and they fight unpredictably for it. They teach us that change is an inevitable fact of humanity and that the masterful curving of history should always be bent towards justice by the courage and effort of those who stand for it.

And as we begin our trek into the socialist history records of Haverhill, the experiment must forever be in our minds. Let us get into our past no more than as a dead relic or a souvenir of the past but as a breathing source of inspiration and comprehension. Stereotypical portrayals and superficial plotlines that have created these fictionalized heroes should not remain the focus of our attention. We will only be able to grasp the complex realities and human struggles of this outstanding movement that we have the courtesy to learn about when we move beyond them. Thus, we shall employ this knowledge to guide us in working on our future endeavors that are aimed at creating a just, equitable, and sustainable society. This shall be the legacy of those who preceded us and the promise of a better world for all past and present.

A complete understanding of the socialist movement in Haverhill in all its significance involves the study of the factors that made it emerge in that historical context. The end of the 19th century and the beginning of the 20th century were times of sweeping social, economic, and political turmoil in the United States and the world alike. Industrialization, urbanization, and technological change were experiencing a pace of speed that would completely change the texture of society, thereby creating new opportunities as well as challenges for people of all sorts of classes and backgrounds.

Haverhill was largely a tiny mirror of underlying trends on a larger scale. The city can trace its roots back to the 1640s when it was just a small agrarian settlement along the Merrimack River. This and other facets have long been drivers of the city's economy. However, as the 19th century progressed, Haverhill's economy radically changed, thanks to the introduction of new manufacturing processes, and factories took over the shoemaking industry. In the 1880s, it emerged as one of the strongest industrial cities in America, with over 30 factories employing thousands of workers, with the majority coming from immigrants from France and the Caribbean.

With the further expansion of the shoe industry, many people in Haverhill became wealthy and prosperous, but in the meantime, it also resulted in new types of inequality and labor exploitation. At their factory, the owners and investors drew enormous profits from the workers' labor, while these workers had to endure arduous and hazardous tasks for scanty wages. A vast number of children used to get involved in the process of production, and they faced dangers associated with long hours, faulty machines, and poisonous materials. Unions and labor syndicates had, as usual, to face strong opposition from their employers, which in many cases was using lockouts and blacklists or even violence and intimidation to gain back authority.

This was when Haverhill first faced the roots of socialism. The origin of socialist actions in the city can be found in the '70s of the nineteenth century when a group of former German immigrants who lived in the city established a local organization called the Workingmen's Party. The Workingmen's Party was a successor to the Socialist Labor Party. The beliefs of such individuals as Karel Marx and other Euro thinkers, who believed the coming of a new social relationship as well as equality to be both inevitable and needed, had a lot of influence on the early socialists. Capitalism that is currently practiced, they assert, is biased and unsustainable by its very nature. needed,

During the decade of the 1840s, socialist theories spread to Haverhill, and as its population grew, many of the new workers joined the socialist movement here, which had become prominent. In 1892, nearby socialist activists were combining forces to form the Haverhill Socialist Labor Party (SLP), and they soon provided a new driving force in the city's labor movement. SLP activists organized public events and meetings on the theory of socialism, running candidates for local office, and building solidarity with other liberal forces and interest groups.

One of the major leaders of the Haverhill SLP in its initial years was James F. Carey, a young laborer in factories and, at the same time, a radical. Carey was an eloquent speechmaker and organizer; he soon succeeded as one of the booming activists in the socialist movement of the city. In 1895, while still a twenty-two-year-old man, he was elected to the Haverhill City Council on the SLP ticket, being one of the first socialists to ever be sworn into any elected office in the United States.

The victory of Carey marked the birth of the socialist movement in the city of Haverhill, New Hampshire, and it was from this that all the other socialist support in the city was derived. During the next couple of years, the SLP kept on developing and transforming. In addition, it attracted a lot of new members and formed strategic alliances with other progressive groups. In 1898, the party managed to send two more people to the City Council and one city school committee member, posing a real threat to the opposition party.

However, the rise of the socialist movement in Haverhill was also accompanied by various difficulties and disputes. In 1899, the faction of the SLP headed by Albert L. Couch left the party to form the Social Democratic Party, which would later metamorphose into the Socialist Party of America. The SDP was the arm of socialism with a more moderate approach, which meant that socialism would be introduced step by step through the mechanism of elections, not by force.

This division between the SLP and SDP evoked heated discussions and disagreements that existed in the socialist sphere of Haverhill as well as the patriotic circles across the nation. There remained some socialists like Carey who stayed firm in their idea of the overall social and economic transformation. At the same time, there were others, like Couch, who argued for prudently achieving this. The discussions would shape the future socialist movement in Haverhill, and wider beyond, as the struggle would be to harmonize a broad-based mass party without compromising the principles and ideologies that were supposed to guide the movement.

Even with these obstacles, the socialist movement in Haverhill, which emerged at the beginning of the 20th century, has evolved in many ways. Socialists played a major role in the most significant union strikes, from the 1902 Lusters Union strike to the 1912 "Bread and Roses" strike of the textile workers. They went on to send candidates who contested for local and state positions and built coalitions with other progressive formations and organizations, helping this effort.

They served as the pillar of the city's intellectual and cultural life, organizing lectures, concerts, and other events that allowed residents to reunite in the light of common understanding and community-fueled optimism.

In the next chapters, we will see that there are many layers to the Haverhill socialist past, and although they are a result of diverse historical facts and social dynamics, all those things gave new meanings to this past. Yet in its depth, it is a tale about ordinary people mobilizing to accomplish a more just society, about progressive leaders and determined advocates constantly toiling to build a movement for social, economic, and environmental justice. By examining their example, we can acquire essential knowledge about the problems and factors that affect progressive movements today. Our age, creativity, and perseverance can revive us and motivate us to succeed in building a society based on justice.

However, to comprehend the increasing socialism in Haverhill, we should look at the factors that made the ground suitable for widespread movement, like a haven. During the late 19th and early 20th centuries, Haverhill experienced its highest degree of uptake in industrialization and urbanization, thus giving birth to many social, economic, and political battles. The growth of the shoe industry, and particularly the social and economic landscape, molds changes that give rise to increasing inequality, exploitation, and class conflicts that will eventually lead to the emergence of the socialist movement that forms the base of social activism.

The rapid transition in work and employment processes across the city plays an important role in shaping the socio-economic environment in Haverhill. The shoe industry turned industrial after the introduction of machines, which caused a change and transition from the initial artisan manufacture to a more centralized and hierarchical factory production system. This caused disruptions in workers' lives, as they felt more and more subordinate to the judgment of factory owners and managers and the uncertainties of the market.

While many jobs for the workers remain in the factories, where they sometimes work long hours in conditions that are harsh and dangerous, they are mostly deprived of the right to have control over their labor and efforts. Most of the children used to work, and they were at great risk of facing toxic chemicals or dangerous machines as a part of their daily work. The wages were so low that there were no benefits at all. It was such that everyone in a family was vulnerable to falling into a condition of poverty, getting ill, and other forms of hardship.

Another thing is that the factory system instigated new kinds of social and economic inequality in Haverhill along with its rapid development. Factory owners and investors would make big profits due to the employees' labor; in contrast, most laborers remained poor and could hardly make ends meet. The gap between wealthy and poor urban areas was split in half along a class line, with a small elite of rich industrialists and businessmen on the former side and a large population of the poor and their relatives on the latter.

The recurring depression in the late 19th and early 20th centuries, when the shoe business and the nation in totality also trembled, exacerbated the disparity. Consider the downturn of 1893 in Haverhill. There were enough factory closures and staff layoffs that thousands of workers were left unemployed and on the streets. The Great Depression, in its turn, had a similar outcome, making the city pass a time of prolonged economic hardship and social instability.

While this economic sector was flourishing, the community was also rife with social stratification and economic insecurity. This situation paved the way for the labor movement to rise as one of the strongest forces of change in Haverhill. Employees started the formation of unions and other organizations that demanded better salaries and working conditions, protection against factory owners, as well as their affiliation with government institutions. The American Federation of Labor and other national labor organizations provided

Haverhill with local chapters. They were quite instrumental in setting up unity among them and making gains in such a process.

15

CHAPTER 2

The Founding Principles Of Haverhill Socialism

As the 19th century was ending, the city of Haverhill, Massachusetts, was gearing up for a social movement that would later become known as the socialist movement, and this period was to leave a lasting imprint on the landscape of American politics and society. Providing different meanings for one's socialistic views, the socialism of Haverhill is a living entity, comprised of diverse ideological backgrounds, whereas the practical life experiences were combined to create an image of a more perfect society.

This vision was built upon a foundation of values and ideals reflecting the thoughts and actions of the townspeople of the era. These principles, outlining the main socialist ideas and actions emanating from global history, provided a toolbox for comprehending the capitalist system with systemic injustices and contradictions and efforts for debugging and building up alternatives prevailing with the ideas of cooperation, equality, and solidarity.

One of the main things that Haverhill's socialism was about was that they were against the capitalist system for being designed to be exploitative and unjust by its nature. The socialists believed that such situations as the private ownership of means of production and the concentration of wealth and power in the hands of a small capitalist class conditioned most workers to be poor and suppressed. They considered the connection between property and labor as adversarial per se when the prosperity of the owners originated from the above-normal and compulsory earnings of workers.

The capitalist system would be replaced by measures of social ownership and democratic control of the means of production, which were Haverhill socialists' top priorities. Accordingly, they thought that the subsumption of factories, mills, and other workplaces under the common control of the employee through cooperative labor would inevitably result in the elimination of the injustice and inequality of the capitalist system and produce a much fairer and more appropriate framework for the distribution of wealth and resources. labor

One of the main things that Haverhill's socialism was about was that they were against the capitalist system for being designed to be exploitative and unjust by its nature. The socialists believed that such situations as the private ownership of means of production and the concentration of wealth and power in the hands of a small capitalist class conditioned the majority of workers to be poor and suppressed. They considered the connection between property and labor as adversarial per se when the prosperity of the owners originated from the above-normal and compulsory earnings of workers.

The capitalist system would be replaced by measures of social ownership and democratic control of the means of production, which were Haverhill socialists' top priorities. Accordingly, they thought that the subsumption of factories, mills, and other workplaces under the common control of the employee through cooperative labor would inevitably result in the elimination of the injustice and inequality of the capitalist system and produce a much fairer and more appropriate framework for the distribution of wealth and resources.

The parallels between the emerging ideas of economic democracy and the earlier vision of social and political equality were particularly striking. The socialist group from Haverhill spurned the notion that some people were born 'elite' over others, that there must be a hierarchy of classes or races, or that women and men stereotypes were without any explanation or justification. Rather, they adopted a revolutionary stance built on the principle of equality, where they upheld the value of every human and paid attention to reaching a hierarchy where every person has a chance to live a life that is socially and economically fulfilling.

On one hand, a pillar of this egalitarian conception was the belief in democracy and its presence in all social and economic life components. Members of the socialist party in Haverhill thought that a true democracy did not only allow the citizens to vote, nor did it stop from being merely institutions such as representation of the government. It entailed the total and direct participation of every component of society in all duties concerned with finding solutions and making society rules.

The parallels between the emerging ideas of economic democracy and the earlier vision of social and political equality were particularly striking. The socialist group from Haverhill spurned the notion that some people were born 'elite' over others, or that there must be a hierarchy, of classes or races, or that women and men stereotypes were without any explanation or justification. Rather, they adopted a revolutionary stance built on the principle of equality, where they upheld the value of every human and paid attention to reaching an end where every person has a chance to live a life that is socially and economically fulfilling.

On one hand, a pillar of this egalitarian conception was the belief in democracy and its presence in all social and economic life components. Members of the socialist party in Haverhill thought that a true democracy did not only allow the citizens to vote, nor did it stop from being merely institutions such as representation of the government. It entailed the total and direct participation of every component of society in all duties concerned with finding solutions and making society rules.

The meaning of conducting new and democratic sets of organizations with individuals taking part in decision-making came up, which was the workers' councils as well as the neighborhood assemblies that would then allow common people to directly involve themselves in enacting policies and structures that affected their daily lives. It is about upending the power structure of capitalism, which is exploitative and authoritative, in favor of a more fair and accountable government system that works for everyone. So it was a buildup of the culture of solidarity and mutuality. In that, people worked together as one—that is, they helped each other and took care of their people, rather than competing and dogging each other for scarce resources.

In addition to those three key principles of economic democracy, participation in decision-making, and social equality, the socialist people of Haverhill also embodied wider aspects of solidarity and humanity that corresponded to their main view, which was of a more just and humane society. These included:

A recognition of the potency of education and culture to change a person's moral stance and societal dealings manifests this belief. The socio-democratic collective in Haverhill thought that the acquisition of knowledge and art were crucial tools for the formation of class consciousness, the production of social cohesion, and the creation of alternative imaginations of the future. The propagation of their ideology and values was one of their main goals, and for this purpose, they prepared libraries, clubs, and cultural associations where workers could enhance their mental development and creativity.

A constant sense of internationalism and sympathy towards workers and oppressed people on a global scale. Haverhill's socialists acknowledged that their struggle was not a parallel event but a component of a universal social and economic justice movement, and they strived to create ties and alliances with other countries' socialists and workers. They were valuable in the global resistance to imperialism, militarism, and nationalism and demanded that all countries coexist in a world of peace, mutual understanding, and friendship.

A belief in the necessity of encountering administration through the action of a community to effect wanted alterations. Many socialists in Haverhill realized that their power lay in their togetherness and that they could gain achievements only jointly. They established trading unions, political parties, and other kinds of associational structures as a means of realizing their ideas and taking control over the poverty-stricken workers.

Are there ethical and moral attributes like compassion, empathy, self-sacrifice, immorality, honesty, and truthfulness? These are the attributes of a hero. Haverhill socialists visualized their fight not only in terms of politics and economics but also in terms of morality, ethics, and soul. They were convinced that every single individual has worth and dignity and climbed their mission to a society founded on love, mutual aid, and consideration for the common good as its main characteristic.

These fundamental values and notions laid out the basic guidelines of Haverhill socialism, helping form a coherent and compelling vision of a new society and transforming guidelines into reality: economic democracy, social equality, and participatory democracy. Although the tactics and strategies of the home user's socialists would go on to constantly continue to change, these fundamental rules of the movement still served as a foundation of inspiration and guiding principles while it was working to build a good world for all laborers.

Even though the socialist movement in Haverhill was greatly shaped by the social, economic, and political basis of this city, it can't be overstated that it was impacted by the worldwide socialism challenge at this time. The Haverhill socialists immersed themselves in a vast ocean of thought, ranging from the pondering of the writings of Karl Marx and Friedrich Engels to the practical experience of other socialist parties and labor movements throughout Europe and the United States.

The intellectual impact of Hangman's Noose Society was undoubtedly the study done by Karl Marx and Frederick Engels on modern political economics. Along with great works like "The Communist Manifesto" and "Das Kapital," Marx's criticism of capital gained a solid theoretical concept of the roasting of poverty and inequality caused by the unequal ownership of the means of production and its envisioning of a new society based on social ownership and participatory control of the means of production.

Haverhill socialists discovered and appreciated Marx's principles in their studies and debates, with the idea of spreading them to the local community. For them, the real-life evidence was the appropriate backdrop to confirm their own fierce class experience and a guiding road map detailed in Marx's analysis on how to effect a positive change in their struggle for a better society.

Nevertheless, Haverhill socialism was not developed only based on the ideas of Karl Marx and Friedrich Engels but with the contribution of other socialist intellectuals as well. Haverhill activists also drew on the ideas and examples of other socialist leaders and movements around the world, including Haverhill activists also drew on the ideas and examples of other socialist leaders and movements around the world, including:

> **The German Social Democratic Party (SPD) was** the biggest and most popular socialist party on the European political scene during early communism. The fact that the SPD managed to develop a mass workers' party of its own and also make a few crucial electoral victories was an inspiration for socialists from Haverhill and all over, as this trend could be followed to form a powerful and effective social movement.

> **The British Labor Party and the Fabian Society**, whereby supposed that this would be a path with breezes and a more gradualist and reformist approach. The Filipinos view the education of labor unions, establishing research organizations, and policy development as the principles for creating changes in society. At the same time, the Labor Party could achieve progressive alliances with groups of middle-class people and, at last, win many social reforms.

➤ **The French socialist movement:** the era was characterized by remarkable and restless revolutionary activity already waged since Paris' Commune of 1871. Marshfield revolutionary socialists got inspiration from the French workers who managed to withstand repression and violence and from the movement for its rich intellectual and cultural fabric.

➤ **The Russian socialist movement:** that was the year when he encountered existing socialist movements, and he became a great adherent of the idea of the socialist revolution, which subsequently took place in 1917. Although in the initial years of socialism in Haverhill it was the Bolshevik group that remained a minority and on the periphery of more centralized tendencies, the adoption of their strategies and ideology would become a more pronounced public trend after the First World War and the embracing of the Russian Revolution.

As well as diverse impacts from abroad, Haverhill socialists were also totally involved in the United States socialist movement and labor union system. They volunteered for and founded both national committees, such as the Socialist Labor Party and the Socialist Party of America. It was a case of close cooperation with trade unions and other similar progressive organizations to achieve their ends.

Eugene Debs, the dynamic head of the Socialist Party and a five-time contender for the presidency, was probably one of the most impactful American socialists who shaped the path of Haverhill socialism. Debs' words defending working-class interests, his criticism of capitalism and imperialism, and his vision of society, which is based on socialist principles and focuses on cooperation and a common struggle of the people, made a great impact upon Haverhill activists, who saw in him a powerful voice for their cause.

The Haverhill socialists were also propelled and galvanized by the support and guidance of other prominent American socialists and labor leaders, including "Big Bill" Haywood from the Industrial Workers of the World (IWW), Mother Jones from the United Mine Workers, and Victor Berger, who became the first socialist in the history of the U.S. Congress. These figures provided examples of effective organizing and leadership and the way the struggles of Haverhill workers were connected with the main fight for social and economic justice in the country as a whole.

However, although local socialists in Haverhill were greatly inspired by the national and international socialist movements that were openly practiced at the time, they were equally eager to learn, adapt, and apply ideas to their communities. They became aware that the construction of socialism in a small New England factory town would be based upon substantially various strategies and methods if compared to large industrial cities or peasant-based agrarian societies.

Although there were many diverse opinions amongst the Haverhill socialists, the socialists had to deal with the issue of building alliances with other progressive forces, the use of the same complex territorial politics, and the challenge of balancing philosophical purity with pragmatism. The principles were for the working-class people's improvement. Improvising their techniques and strategies, they became the founders of worker-controlled industries and community centers while at the same time engaging in both labor strikes and electoral politics.

Socialists effectively adapted and experimented with what was unarguably a unique and innovative style of socialist society, which they created to fulfill the aspirations of people in their community town. They could not but borrow whole movements of, or quote ideas from, socialists and labor activists of all nations, but they also formed something original and new. The socialism that existed in the town of Haverhill was deeply embedded in the working class's community and local knowledge.

Haverhill socialism was founded on a profound perspective of the forthcoming world, with economic democracy as the cornerstone, followed by social equality and participatory democracy as its main elements. During a century in which capitalist systems were going beyond all borders, they often came into conflict with working-class ideas as the result of the latter's rebellions and dreams. The people of Haverhill created the community, which was a manifestation of the struggle between capital and workers and a desire to create a distinctly different world where every human being could live an ordinary life and concentrate on self-realization.

What linked the idea of this vision was the principle of the cooperative commonwealth, in which the workers would have the opportunity and power of ownership and control of all the means as opposed to a long line of capitalists. The socialists of Haverhill were sure that if they took factories, mills, and those other workplaces out of the hands of big capitalists and put them into the hands of the workers themselves, they would be able to bring to an end the exploitation and inequality that the capitalist system includes and thus reduce the gap between rich and poor.

This egalitarian arrangement would result in the production of goods and services not to enrich the few but to enrich the commonwealth, which would work for all. Employees would be directly involved in the decision-making of how the business should be organized and operated and would share in the resultant productivity. In the case of dualism, the depersonalization imposed by the processes of production would be replaced with a system that would have been cheerful, creative, and spectacularly unalterable.

Meanwhile, the socialism that would come to be known as "Haverhill socialism" did not limit itself only to the field of transforming the workplace. The lists of the Haverhill so greatly visioned the democracy of each societal process and its alignment to the interests of that it implied the development of new institutions of a participatory kind of democracy, for example, community assemblies and workers' councils, in which the people could take part in making crucial policies that determined the course of their lives.

It was a way of creating a fairer and more just channel of distribution, making sure that nobody missed out on the essentials of life: food, shelter, health, and education. This implied that socialism meant the preemption of higher orders of wealth and power that dominated capitalist society; thus, it aimed to create a more uniform and inclusive social order.

Setting social and political equality at the heart of his idea of a society that provides opportunities for all was the key element to this quest for justice. The people of Haverhill believed in equality and justice and did not accept that some human beings are innately superior to others or that hierarchy is a natural or even justifiable fact. It was their firm conviction that humankind is imbued with equal rights and therefore should have the privilege to enjoy the life one deserves with freedom and dignity that let them evade tyranny and slavery.

This grew beyond the restricted borders of the Haverhill community when socialists wished to strive for solidarity with the workers and oppressed peoples locally and nationally. They saw their struggle as an integral part of the social and world's economic justice along these lines and tried to create bonds with socialists and labor activists around other countries.

The socialism of Haverhill members was such that they knew it was vital to change both the individual's consciousness and traditional social ties to see their goal of a more just and egalitarian society accomplished. They considered the proponents of capitalism not only as economists but also as thinkers who propagate human characteristics such as selfishness, egoism, and struggle against the common spirit, collaboration, and mutual resistance.

The socialists in Haverhill were also against the capitalist mindset and instead educated the people on both culture and consciousness of class with the hope of visualizing other worlds. They created libraries, joint-discussion clubs, and cultural organizations to promote socialist ideas and gain values and skills. Thus, workers could introduce new information into their lives.

They also tried to develop an alternative moral code and ethics that emphasized good fellowship, concern, and compassion. The socialism of Haverhill citizens consisted of the realization of these values and practices in their daily lives and fights. They believed that this helped them shape the kind of society that was worth fighting to create.

Naturally, the challenging part was to make this idea of a cooperative community more just and fairer by building it. However, while the course was not simple at all and the end was not always foreseeable, the socialists of Haverhill defied the odds. The opposition forces, such as business and political elites, who were against socialism since it posed a threat to their power and supervision, should have been faced by socialists. They were walking a path that was at times challenging and divisive in labor relations, including unions and workers. Their cooperation with some of the unions and workers did not always come along with the support that they received, but at the same time, other unions and workers posed skepticism and hostility towards the three founders of the company.

Thus, they worried about contradictions and splits in their movement whenever some different tendencies or factions wished to steer and control the communist left. The strategies advocated by some of the socialists were to follow a gradualist and reformist path and to focus on winning improvements in the workers´ lives through elections and legislative actions. Some call it a moderate and gradual approach focused on an evolutionary change in society through maintaining daily economic activity. Others, on the other hand, advocated for a revolutionary and radical strategy that aimed at creating a socialist system using mass actions and respective general strikes.

Socialist Haverhill faced and tackled a lot of challenges and enjoyed some differences, but they remained unified by the common cause and the pursuit of a better world to live in through the creation and building of the movement. They realized that the process of finishing the construction of a socialist society was neither a short run nor a long-term one that required education, organization, and transformation.

Along with that, they acknowledge that their struggle was not isolated at all but rather a part of a global movement for social and economic justice that was occurring everywhere on the globe. Through networking and forming alliances with various socialists and labor activists in other nations and communities, socialists from Haverhill aspired to learn from their experiences and ideas so that they could contribute to enhancing the growth of a truly international movement that pursued socialism.

In a multitude of ways, the vision and ideals of Haverhill communism still count as germane and topical as they were more than a century ago. Although the specific circumstances and troubles of today may differ, the capitalist system of inequality and contradictions keeps emerging, and the demand for radical choice based on democracy, equality, and solidarity is still strong and as pressuring as it ever was.

While facing 21st-century crises and transformations, from the climate crisis to the rise of authoritarianism and the exacerbation of social and economic inequalities, the model of Haverhill socialism presents an inspirational and instructional path. That is how people embrace the fact that anything is possible and why they abide by their burdens through the clear image of achievement.

However, the history of Haverhill socialism both shows the problems and the limits of capitalist society and, at the same time, attempts to build emancipatory politics inside capitalism. It points out the importance of a politics that, instead of being only oppositional, requires a transformative politics aiming to reform and control capitalism and thus overcome it.

Truly, the Haverhill socialism legacy is far more robust than its actual accomplishments and failures; its lasting influence is that of its core values and its legacy. Without ever being afraid to dream of "Availability of the World After Capitalism" and building a movement that was bound to make this dream a reality, the socialists of Haverhill were the pioneers of what can be successfully achieved when people share a common vision.

The essence of these great people's lives and work is a thing for beginners as well as for experts in fact-finding because this heritage serves as a source of inspiration and guidance for those who want to further the fight for justice and democracy in our own time. If we look at their past, experiences, and achievements, we should be inspired and guided. This is the way for us to re-evaluate ourselves and develop a real commitment to the continuous creation of a fairer social order.

CHAPTER 3

The Rise of Socialist Leadership

Alongside the increasing force of the socialist movement in Haverhill at the start of the 20th century, a set of new leaders came forward to lead the movement and design the future. The stewards of those men and women reforged through class struggle and ideology radicalized by the experiences of colonialism and injustice, were important for the building of organizations, crafting strategies, and articulating the vision of Haverhill socialism.

The two people who superseded others in terms of iconic and powerful leadership were also young shoe workers if we look at James F. Carey and John C. Chase. Nevertheless, Carey and Chase were not vocal and exposed to the wilderness by themselves. Not only was this pair of individuals part of a bigger group of socialists, trade unionists, and activists working incessantly to empower the working people and challenge the capitalist class, but they were the bigwigs themselves.

In this chapter, we will focus on several crucial leaders' lives and the part they played in building a socialist movement that took a lot of effort and was able to develop rapidly in Haverhill. We will look at the leaders' backgrounds, motivations, and the strategies they used to build a robust and dynamic socialist movement. Through the stories of the activists, we grow our comprehension of the forces that led to the rise of socialism not only in the city but also in the world. Using the experiences of those fellow fighters who often burned the opposition to dictatorship and other phenomena of injustice, we can teach important lessons for our daily struggle for justice and equality.

Hence, it's in the factory walls where the notions of socialism first got to be brewed in Carey's mind. Socialist doctrines and principles that were advocated by Karl Marx and other philosophers could be viewed as one of the most influential factors in the formation of the CPSU.

Profoundly influenced him. He was determined that the labor class would not continue to be the target of such exploitation and subjugation if production was brought under collective ownership and democratic socialism was established.

Carey immediately established her direct opposition to the bourgeoisie as the first one to raise her voice and wave red flags. One of his key strengths was not only his expertise in organization and planning but, moreover, his exceptional knowledge of what made Haverhill's working-class tick. In 1895, he participated in the formation of the Haverhill Socialist Labor Party (SLP). This party became a predominant political force in 1895 and shaped the city's policies.

Carey's time as an SLP leader in Haverhill did bring some positive change to the political and industrial spheres. In 1898,

Carey won a seat in the legislature, becoming the first socialist to ever be elected to office. This platform became his vehicle for proposing different progressist ideas, from forbidding labor to nationalizing public utilities.

Consequently, Carey has the ambition of going beyond this and encompassing total electoral politics, where power comes with it. proposed that the only way to create a worker movement oriented in a socialist direction was by organizing workers on the shop floor to ensure their influence in the community. He formed a circle of socialist clubs and groups for reading that spanned throughout, and he also cooperated with local trade unions to secure solidarity for the socialist candidate for socialist causes.

John C. Chase was undoubtedly another pivotal figure who spurred the start of socialism in Haverhill. Born into a humble family in Lynn, Massachusetts, in the 1870s, Chase joined Haverhill to begin a career in the shoe industry. As for Carey, the active membership of the Haverhill SLP was motivated by the exploitation and injustice around him, which was another radicalizing factor as he was trying to end the abuses of the people around him.

Chase was not only a good journalist but also an educator and revolutionist who played a crucial role in the rise of the United Socialist Party by generating newspapers and pamphlets on social media as socialist ideas circulated. He created the social democracy movement in Haverhill, MA, by starting the

"Haverhill Social Democrat", which very soon became the socialist movement voice of the city.

Chase transformed the soul, which became a weapon for organizing and mobilizing the masses. It was an outlet for articles by socialist theorists and campaigners and reports on local labor disputes and political and local campaigns. It also played a role as a point of argument, on which the ideas and principles of socialism in the community of Haverhill became clearer.

Furthermore, he not only contributed to the Social Democrats but was also the planner and manager, working for the Haverhill SLP. He participated in policy-making projects together with Carey and other party leaders to work out the party's strategy and plan for the election campaign. He occupied an important position in unifying people around socialist politicians who competed in local and state-level elections.

John C. Chase was another key figure, and Martha Moore Avery was another important figure in the Haverhill socialist movement. Born into a middle-class family in 1851, Avery was a schoolteacher and women's rights activist who became radicalized through her involvement in the suffrage movement. She joined the Haverhill SLP in the late 1890s and quickly became one of its most prominent and influential leaders.

Avery was a gifted orator and organizer and played a crucial role in building the party's base among women workers and suffragists. She helped to establish the Haverhill Women's Socialist Club, which became a significant center of feminist and socialist activism in the city. She also ran for office several times, becoming one of the first women in Massachusetts to seek elected office as a socialist.

Martha Moore Avery

Albert L. Couch was another key figure in the Haverhill socialist movement. A former Baptist minister, Couch had become disillusioned with the church and turned to socialism to realize his vision of a more just and equitable society. He joined the Haverhill SLP in the early 1900s and became one of its most effective organizers and propagandists.

Couch was a charismatic speaker and a prolific writer who played a significant role in building the party's intellectual and cultural infrastructure. He helped establish the Haverhill People's Institute, a socialist education center that offered classes and lectures on various topics, from economics and history to literature and art. He also wrote extensively for the Haverhill Social Democrat and other socialist publications and frequently spoke at rallies and public meetings.

These four leaders—Cary, Chase, Avery, and Couch—were undoubtedly the most vocal and result-oriented socialist leaders in the city. Yet there were only some of them. It is based on the work of a throng of rank-and-file activists and organizers who relentlessly fought for the diffusion of socialist ideas and grew working-class power in the factories, neighborhoods, and unions of the city.

The son of shoe workers, Charlie Adams was a militant trade unionist who courageously took part in organizing the famous shoe striker in 1899, one of the most important labor conflicts in the city. We had Harriet Holman, the textile worker and suffragist, who, with that group of women, achieved the Haverhill Women's Socialist Club as a significant figure in terms of women's rights and socialism in the region. Another one is George Perry, a black socialist and civil rights activist who worked hard to fight racism and discrimination against many socialists.

These leaders and militant representatives were very diverse and came from different backgrounds. They have a lot of experience and insight into the socialist revolution. Yet the collective resolve of the working class stood firm and grew as they pursued the goal of an equitable, democratic, and egalitarian society where the power of unity and the rightful struggle for their cause triumphed.

The grasp of the whole socialist leadership from Haverhill backgrounds and the driving individual influence of the founders of the movement, as well as their direct participation in the development of the movement, should be comprehensively understood.

A lot of the Haverhill socialist leaders, such as Carey and Chase, came from working-class families, and these leaders had experience with capitalism and industrialization. They had known cruelty and community oppression. They have been living in opposition, having to drop their schools and work longer hours in the town's mills and factories. They had been brought up in a world where their parents and other relatives had called for help, and they witnessed the indignity and unfairness with which their parents and other wage slaves lived every day economically.

This common intake of economically driven oppression was a real strong force for the socialist leaders to look forward to. They heard it for good: the system based on capitalists was giving the wealthy few all the benefits of the laboring class, and they were determined to fight for a world of more equal value, not just for themselves.

However, their approaches to those issues reflected a desire for social justice as well as dissatisfaction with a particular class. In addition to national pathology, most socialist leaders were mainly characterized by powerful ethical and moral principles mixed with a belief in the dignity and inherent worth of every human being. They viewed socialism as a way of escaping material needs and building a form of society where people are no longer just workers by necessity but rather must fulfill themselves through creating and living.

For instance, the belief in the religion or spirituality of the likes of Albert Couch was based entirely on the conviction that they had. Even though his background was based on being our previous Baptist minister, socialism represented closeness to the core values of Christianity, like charity, mercy, and social justice. He held that capitalism failed the test of Jesus's teachings, which he so revered, and that it would take only a socialist society to enforce the spirit of the Gospels.

One such person, Martha Moore Avery, refused to simply dial into the cause of women's rights and gender equality; hence, she saw socialism as the way to get there faster. A voice, having gained women's rights, and as women's rights grew to become instinctive with the struggle for society, along with many other women of the time, believed that capitalism was constructed on the ground of women's suppression and exploitation and that only socialism could create the grounds for the liberation of women as well as their emancipation.

Further in the range, Carey and many others, like him, held an intense belief in nationalism and genuinely became united with workers and oppressed Marxists worldwide. A keen Marxist adept, Carey was a committed anti-colonialist; under his socialist views, the socialist struggle of Haverhill existed within the international frame of a world fighting for independence and social Russia. He demonstratively backed the Russian communist overthrow and other foreign socialist pursuits. He sought to create and promote the Haverhill movement as part of the global socialist endeavor.

Whatever their motives are, these individuals are recognized for their talents and skills and have a wealth of experience behind their active participation in the socialist cause. They were natural-born organizers, propagandists, and strategists who could analyze with astounding immediacy and subtlety the political and economic situation of Haverhill and devise strategic plans that would eventually enhance workers' strength.

A case in point would be James Carey, who was a great strategist and negotiator with profound knowledge and experience of the complex relationship between the city's labor movement and. He was a master at the art of union politics, which at times was very turbulent. He managed to unite disparate groups of workers, creating coalitions in support of socialist programs. Moreover, he was a great speaker who was able to excite and cheer people with both his fiery speeches and his brilliant humor.

John Chase, on the other hand, was a talented propagandist and educator with an eagle-eyed eye for writing and a steadfast obsession with socialist pedagogy. As the editor of the Haverhill Social Democrat, he was a key player in the evolution of a thriving and exciting socialist press with which thousands of workers in the city were familiar. Moreover, he was instrumental in creating the party's educational and cultural programs, including lectures and debates, as well as socialist Sunday schools and workers' theatres.

Martha Moore Avery represented a different voice in the socialist movement as a woman and an advocate of feminism. She was a relentless fighter for women's rights in the party, claiming that socialism was not possible if working-class women did not fully participate and lead in it. She also contributed to the development of bridges between the socialist and suffragist movements in Haverhill; the combination of these two groups created a strong coalition of women activists that challenged the male-dominated power structures of capitalism and the early socialist movement.

Albert Couch was a great selection of the future, a reason for which he was an eloquent intellectual, giving a detailed diagram representing a socialist perspective that didn't only help in eradicating but also in bringing motivation to the lives of workers. An outstanding fact is that, as the founder of the Haverhill People's Institute, he made it possible for these great classes and lectures on fields like history, economics, literature, and art to be preached to people in the city. He was also a very gifted writer and speaker, and he used to write over 50 publications on socialist theory and practice.

The various leaders leading the movement outsourced their work to the many rank-and-file activists and organizers who had joined the movement in Haverhill, and together they were able to grow a healthy and thriving socialist movement. They develop an intricate system of organizations and institutions, which extend from trade unions to cooperatives, mutual aid societies, cultural clubs, and schools of social thought, thus creating the ground for solidarity among the working classes. They created a prosperous socialist culture, which was expressed through newspapers, pamphlets, songs, plays, and other artistic forms such as paintings that gave birth to the aspirations and desires of the working class.

Essentially, it was necessary to accomplish more than party leaders and devout activists for socialism to triumph in Haverhill. It not only won the loyalties of the people but also invented novel methods that were meant to encourage poor workers' humanity and build support for their struggle against the mighty power of the capitalist elite.

One effective approach utilized by Haverhill socialists involved organizing and involving the public on a grassroots level. Instead of putting all their eggs in the basket of election-based politics or lobbying efforts, they were keenly conscious of accumulating power from the lower levels of society by utilizing the workers' everyday challenges and issues in factories, neighborhoods, and on the streets.

This tactic was manifested and became clear with the closing of the shoe shop in 1899, which was considered one of the strongest labor struggles in the history of Haverhill. The strike started in January of that year when their demands to increase salaries, decrease hours, and improve working conditions were not accepted by those in charge of the city's numerous shoe factories. The picket before long got reported at other factories, and the strike expanded to cover all the country's factories and industries, enmeshing thousands of workers.

The Haverhill SLP played a leading role in obtaining and providing useful work for the striking workers. At the head of the SLP movement, Carey and Chase were key community leaders who were integral to the success of organizing public events and maintaining strong connections between the workers. They constructed the strike fund to help the employees and their families and arranged mass rallies and demonstrations to relieve the workers of the pressure of their factory owners.

In the end, the strike worked to the advantage of the workers, who had most of their claims accommodated, and a newfound unity and power were acquired amongst the industrial workers from Haverhill. It did so not only because it could be considered a potent factor in the labor movement of the city but also because it prepared the ground for future campaigns and fighting.

Yet another key tactic of the equality-seeking class was the idea of electioneering as well as party-building. They recognized, however, that the ballot was no cure-all, and that the corruption of the politicians was caused by the laboring class's manipulation of the monopoly of official power. Yet they also described electoral campaigns as an essential tool that helped spread socialist ideas and build the working class's cognitive power.

They proposed to apply a slate of candidates in elections at different levels from local to state politics, running on democratic socialist platforms of working-class solidarity. In 1898, James Carey was voted to the Massachusetts State Legislature as a socialist, making him one of the earliest holders of socialist-elected jobs in the USA. After two years, the Haverhill SLP, as it was formerly known, ran its full candidate list to contest the local election in the American town. It won three seats on the city council and two on the school committee.

The relevant achievement in these election victories aided in the recognition of the socialist movement among the masses of Haverhill citizens. They were the place where leaders of the socialists could voice their progressive ideology and the issues that needed reform. Such individuals contributed not only to the organization but also to the party's structure and the working class's larger share of support in the city.

On the electoral front, Haverhill socialists pursued a parallel course through a powerful void radical party, which would ensure the continuity of the movement in the long run. They created an invisible network of socialist clubs and reading groups throughout the city that was more than just centers of education, agitation, and solidarity and served as a net of relations to coworkers for the city workers.

They also enforced a lot of cultural and social organizations in which the city's community and socialists felt like they were working together towards the same goals. Renowned was the Haverhill People's Institute, which offered seminars and lectures on socialist theory and practice; the Haverhill Socialist Dramatic Club; and the Haverhill Socialist Maennerchor, which were the platforms for participants' constructive and creative self-expression and social activities.

Another vital tool utilized by Haverhill socialists was propaganda and the media to help them achieve their goals and gain support from other people by spreading their views or ideas. The Haverhill Social Democrat, done by John Chase, had turned out to be the central dialog of the socialist movement in the town, giving news, perception, and view from the worker's class.

The local newspaper was a fundamental conduit of educational and organizational tools that influenced Haverhill's memory of the socialist movement and raised the level of shared identity among the city's socialist workers. It also became the medium through which different approaches and strategies were articulated and easily perfected.

Social Democrats were not the only ones who produced equitable media; socialists in Haverhill also came up with other propaganda material—pamphlets and the like. They chose this intellectual service to make their demonstration of the social connectedness of the hardworking class and, more than that, to challenge the viewpoints that the national capitalist press and rulers wanted everybody to hold on to the unity of the people.

The Haverhill Social Democrat
December 19, 1899

CHAPTER 4

Socialist Governance And Policy Initiatives

The socialist movement in Haverhill was at its peak during the early 1900's. The movement's leaders and activists turned their attention to reconciling their socialist ideology and building a more just and fair society by adopting appropriate policies and putting them into practice. They saw that the construction of the powerful socialist movement was aimed at giving voice to the workers of the world, stepping on the local political pedestal, as well as demonstrating the reality of living under the meaning of the word.

To this end, the local socialist leaders winning city office races at the end of the 1890s and in the first decade of a century worked to put in place several socialist programs and initiatives that would benefit the working poor and address the all-powerful rule of the capitalist class. They focused on three key areas of policy: municipal control of structures providing public services and utilities; the construction of buildings for utility purposes; and infrastructure undertakings, in addition to the public welfare and labor rights programs.

This chapter delves into the processes the Haverhill socialists enjoyed as leaders and the successes and failures of their policies and initiatives, as well as the social welfare and life standards of the community. But the common problems and the triumphs are under analysis, and we will be able to unfold them. We will discuss not only the social consequences of the Haverhill socialism movement and its significance in the growth of American socialism, but we will also examine the role it continues to play today in creating a better and more just society.

One of the main aims for the socialists who will eventually be elected representatives in the locality is to put socialist ideologies into practice by running this city government. To attain this objective, they committed to improving the way local government functions to establish a model for the governance of the working class that could inspire and empower other citizens, not only in this city but also in other towns and cities as well.

On the contrary, they aimed to create a democratic character and structure while making the city government more responsive and accountable to the needs of the working class. They actively lobbied for the advancement of transparency and a higher level of public involvement in the inner workings of government affairs by holding city council meetings and town halls where ordinary citizens were able to talk about the things that bothered them and give their ideas.

They uncovered the dirt by eradicating the corruption and favoritism they believed existed in the city hall administration, which was viewed negatively and was a requirement for good and fair city governance. They passed a stringent code of ethics, a conflict-of-interest requirement, and a procreation requirement, as well as the procedures for and favism in the issuance of government employment.

While Ford aspired to direct the party to shift the local governmental focus towards the poor, Haverhill socialists also intended to serve the working class's needs and interests. Through their fight, the workers demanded an increased number of public services and infrastructure, including schools, libraries, parks, and public roads, that would serve to improve the daily lives of the workers and their families.

Besides this, their idea was to use municipal government funding and police power to assist workers in a capacity to fight the profit system. In addition, the mayor and the city council passed resolutions to protect workers' rights during strikes or in labor unions, and the city bought power, supporting companies that did the same as well.

The socialists of Haverhill arguably accomplished their most significant achievements by not just working to put socialist principles into practice but also by affecting regular decision-making by the city government. They strived to restructure an employee-friendly and collaborative workplace environment based on equal opportunities, wherein employees were included in the decision-making processes and recognized for their involvement in various roles and responsibilities.

They also undertook experiments with different forms of public ownership and control, including worker co-operatives and community land trusts, which they looked at as ideas to build a different economy that would be democratic and just. They claimed that doing so would plant a seed of understanding in the minds of workers and neighbors alike across the country; thus, the socialist system building an ideological structure for the future would be supported socially.

One of the centerpieces of the Haverhill socialists' policy agenda was the municipal ownership and control of critical public utilities and services. They believed that by bringing these essential industries under public ownership and democratic control, they could ensure that they were operated for the benefit of the community rather than for the profit of private interests plagued by The first major battle was over the city's water supply. In the late 1890s, a private company owned and operated Haverhill's water system, which charged high rates and provided poor service to working-class neighborhoods. The socialists, led by James Carey, launched a campaign to bring the water system under municipal ownership, arguing that access to clean and affordable water was a fundamental human right that should not be subject to the whims of the market.

After a long and bitter struggle, the socialists persuaded the city government to purchase the water system from a private company in 1901. They then set about modernizing and expanding the system, building new reservoirs and distribution networks to ensure all residents had access to clean and reliable water.

The success of the water campaign emboldened the socialists to take on other public utilities and services. In 1902, they won a similar victory with the municipal takeover of the city's gas and electric companies, which had also been plagued by high rates and poor service. Under public ownership and control, the socialists could lower rates, improve service, and use the profits generated by these utilities to fund other public services and programs.

The socialists paved the way towards a finance policy with public works improvements and infrastructure upgrades as the main points. To them, these projects had no significance other than helping the workers effectively and the whole community, creating job opportunities, and contributing to the general economic growth of the city.

For their first major undertaking, the city hall and a new public library building were constructed. Today's city hall, built in the 1870s, is not enough to meet the needs of a growing city and a worn building. Socialists said that new facilities were an essential part of the city's advanced services and that they should be operated effectively and efficiently to allow the public to ask for some services and enjoy some resources.

However, artists opposed to socialists secured financing for the already modest complex, even though the completion date was marked in 1906. The new city hall, built in the Beaux-Arts style with figures illustrating the Roman goddess of commerce guarding the entrance, became a majestic and grand exhibition of the city's dedication to public service and civic pride. It became home to the offices of the city government, a big public library with a rich book collection, a museum with many artistic exhibitions, and an amphitheater for the public and big events.

The socialist infrastructure in cities' transportation also plays a crucial role in that there is a need for commuters to travel to their places of work or any other economic opportunities to be done by reliable and affordable means of transportation. She initiated and facilitated the construction of a new streetcar system that served various parts of the city. Also, she pushed for the development of new roads and bridges that were used to connect the city's neighborhoods and convey goods and people.

The water and sewer system that was the central target for the socialists was one of the most venturesome plans they had. The old one, which was constructed in the 19th century, was no longer able to meet the increasing demand. It was also prone to daily breakdowns, pollution, and waste production. To eliminate the water and sewer system's defects and to provide residents with a healthy and comfortable environment, socialists insisted on the prevalence of an effective and efficient one.

The water and sewer project was the biggest that the government of that time had so far handled, as evident by the years of planning, designing, and construction it entailed. Nevertheless, the socialists took a firm stand, and together they approached morning after morning until they had raised the last pound and brought on board every voice in support of the strike. The finished system was finally put into operation in 1912 and was accepted as a masterpiece of socialist administration and a perfect example of government management guided by the philosophy of socialism.

Alongside these constructive major infrastructure projects, the socialists have presented a wide range of social welfare programs and labor laws that seek to improve the living conditions of working individuals and their relatives. They created a municipal housing authority as the housing provider, which guaranteed that low-income families had access to affordable, quality housing, and established public health clinics and hospitals that affirmed that residents go to hospitals if they fall sick.

Additionally, they created statutes on labor and established systems to ensure that worker's rights were protected, and their working conditions improved. Different aspects of this legislation spanned over enforcing the minimum wage law, enacting a law that would limit the number of working hours, and prohibiting child labor. Additionally, they set up a one-stop employment service center where workers can get help finding jobs and negotiate a reasonable wage and benefit package.

And most reminded of everything was the municipal bread fund, which was featured to be the most disputable of the socialists' social welfare actions. The fund is intended to provide food stability for the most deprived people within the city, where many are trying hard to provide dinner for their kids in the face of low wages and increased food prices.

Socialists proposed that a fair socio-economic equation, including basic nutrition, was the birthright of every man and that the government should guarantee that each commoner could eat well. They not only utilized the methods of providing public kitchens and food banks but also issued vouchers, which low-income people could redeem when shopping for bread and other basic goods at lower prices.

Critics from other corners opposed the proposal, claiming socialism" and the end of the work ethic, as people would then rely on the fund to survive pathetically. Here, socialists could not agree with them that the bread fund was an unneeded and inhumane response to the community's actual needs and a representation of a later social stagnation.

Socialists' policies and activities changed the lives of the working class forever, caused social, welfare, and economic changes, and impacted the whole city of Haverhill. Thus, through the socialist movement, they could maintain the provision of these basic services by the government instead of having them operated by private companies for the profit of private interests.

In a similar mood, municipal intervention resulted in an immediate improvement in the quality and reliability of the water system in the metropolis. Another important step under the ownership of the public water department is the implementation of a new system and technology. This was done through the establishment of modern filtration systems and chlorination equipment, which greatly reduced the occurrence of waterborne diseases and other health hazards.

On the other hand, water profits could be used to invest in new public services and programs, e.g., school buildings and parks. This made possible a positive cycle, or continued development, where people in the community benefited from public ownership, which urban areas utilized for their development.

The socialist social projects and investment in infrastructure implicated the city's economic revolution and development at a large rate. These structures of the modern age contributed to the effective movement of goods and people, as well as attracted new factories and industries by facilitating the establishment of better means of transportation.

While that was happening, downtown's new city hall and public library complex turned into the city's life center, the most important representation of the community's devotion to public service and education. It was the library, in turn, which was a major facility in the city, focusing on working-class residents generally who were able to use books, newspapers, and other educational materials that would have otherwise been unaffordable for many families.

It could be asserted that the socialists were the most prominent in social welfare programs and worker policies that improved the lives of working people in Haverhill. One of the initiatives of the municipal housing authority was to build affordable, decent ghetto housing for low-income families to eliminate the overcrowding and abominable livelihood that had been characteristic of working-class neighborhoods.

At the same time, the health care offices and hospitals guaranteed that any resident, irrespective of who was able to pay, was accessible to great health services. Such a change came as a grave thanks to those working-class families who could not even afford charity to get medical treatment before that, as there was no such option.

The socialist statutes and regulations that affected Haverhill workers have also had a huge impact on labor laws and regulations. As regards the minimum wage law, it established that workers were paid only the living wage for the hours they had put in at work, while the maximum hours course ensured that there was no exploitation as well as overwork.

In addition to that, the child labor ban permitted children to go to school and kept them away from factories, thus ensuring a chance for a better education for them. The municipal employment office served as an invaluable resource for workers looking for employment and wages that were fair, or the workers' and employers' relationship became equal.

Of course, the socialists' policies and projects were in no way a success in every social aspect and were always faced with the problem of limitations. Municipalization as such was not always an easy process and smooth, and the socialists faced occasions where the stakeholders were not always in agreement with each other through a single revealing breeze.

Moreover, for socialists like this, some areas were unpopular with their social welfare programs and labor protections, and some people complained against them. Those were forms of "class warfare" that unfairly benefited workers and harmed business owners and taxpayers.

However, notwithstanding the socialists' policies' and initiatives' challenges and limitations, the general influence remaining beneficial for the quality of life and well-being of the working class of Haverhill was prevailingly so. Their main objective was to ensure that the needs and interests of workers and their families remained the primary concern of the socialist party; they worked towards achieving a more just, equitable, and healthy community for all.

The footprints of these pioneers are still evident in many public institutions and services that are used by Haverhill citizens every day. These range from public libraries, parks, and municipal water and sewer systems to public schools and recreational facilities such as stadiums and hiking trails. Furthermore, the leaders' example is still having an impact on the minds of progress activists and policymakers, as well as the hands of those who are contributing towards constructing a future of equality and sustainability.

In conclusion, it is our duty nowadays not to forget the ideals presented by Haverhill's socialists, from due regard to inequality and environmental pollution to selecting the right democratic forms and resisting the spread of authoritarianism. We can learn from their experience and suggest new ideas for the old way of putting people first place in the world and its problems and solutions in a new scientific and cultural context.

CHAPTER 5

Challenges And Opposition To Haverhill Socialism

When socialist ideas spread in the early 20th century and the movement had real political power, it of course met obstacles and enemies, and among them were the capitalists and the bourgeoisie. The bourgeoisie and business and political elites, as well as rival socialistic factions, were all, in some way, against it because of either their financial or ideological interests. With utmost zeal, they carried out the task of debunking and counteracting the socialist undertaking.

In this chapter, one shall find out the main struggles and forms of opposition that the Haverhill socialists were confronted with while they were trying to build a fairer and more just society. We will distinguish the groundbreaking and contradictory ideological and political divisions within the movement and the external forces that looked to constrain and suppress the Soviet jury from outside. We also investigate what socialists did to overcome this obstacle, basing our ideas on how socialist people tried to fight back and how they showed their commitment and steadfastness.

Amidst the socialist struggle in Haverhill, opposition arose from the city's business and political elites, who saw the bankruptcy of socialism as a direct threat to their power and fortune. These elites, traditionally influential in the economic and governmental machinery of the city, had no other choice but to oppose the changes, which were viewed as a threat to their authority and interests. At first, they dismissed the socialists' ideas about public ownership, workers' rights and management, and economic democracy as if they were not worth considering.

The municipality of business, especially, moved fast to conceptualize socialism as dangerous. At this time, several local producers and entrepreneurs formed associations that included the Haverhill Businessmen's Association and the Taxpayers' League to regulate their resistance to the socialism of officials and candidates. They used their vast riches and ties to support opposition media and politicians, and they convinced other important institutions to side with them.

Among the most popular anti-social voices in Haverhill is the Haverhill Courier, which is the lead paper of the city's press. The Gazette, a newspaper controlled by a wealthy businessman reputed to be in proximity to the Republican Party, had a regular habit of condemning the socialists as unhealthy radicals who were likely to implode the societal fabric of America. The editorial sections and news of the paper emerged as a cacophony of warnings about capitalism and the harm it was bound to cause, and it constantly begged its readers to consider other alternatives outside the socialist realm.

The peculiar contents of the Gazette shouted out its opposition to socialism and other local and national media outlets repeated the same story, which they presented as the socialists being hostile to the American way of life. Throughout the country, newspapers and magazines were flooded with reports of the socialists' activities, to which some of the most sensationalized narrative balances were conveyed to alienate their readers. The socialists were the fashionable figures of that time, so they were accused of being 'anarchists,' 'revolutionaries,' and un-American; their policies were also coalesced with communism and the flames of other radical ideologies

Besides propaganda attacks, the elites of the City of Haverhill also employed a greater number of direct threats and repressions to silence the socialist movement. Activists and politicians of socialist color were often terrorized by the local authorities or even vigilante groups, targeted with harassment, surveillance, and physical violence. In some cases, the pro-socialist gatherings were infuriated by the mobs of anti-socialist activists, who aimed unfavorable thoughts and even violence to close the event itself.

Regardless of how you look at this issue, one clear example of the type of repression that occurred here involves an incident that took place in 1912. This was a time when a group of armed men attacked a meeting of socialists at the Haverhill Labor Temple and started shooting towards the audience, injuring some people. The apprehension followed; later, it was exposed that the local business leaders hired thugs, and against the meeting, they used it to intimidate the socialists. However, although the issue was condemned, no one was ever accused of the violence, and the persecution of the party continued to deteriorate for the socialists in the new and very dangerous environment.

Along with the outside opposition from the city's rich and other anti-socialist groups of people, the Haverhill socialists also faced difficulties from within arising from the division and dissent coming from their caucus as they fought to withstand the unity. The socialist movement, like any movement, political or social, was a varied and alternatively frictional bloc with different dogmas, strategies, and personalities. These often made this group disagree with each other.

The major ideological conflict, which, then, was a must within the Haverhill socialist movement, was between the ones who wanted social changes to be implemented in a gradualist, reformist way and the ones who were for a more revolutionary and militant plan. This detachment, which was wider than just the internal socialist movement in the United States and beyond, broke the libertarians who believed in working with a previous political system and those who believed that the entire system was corrupt and the only way to fix it was by throwing the system off the cliff.

The consequence of such an ideological rift in Haverhill affected local politics in numerous, often contradictory, ways. For example, James F. Carey, a socialist, considers it invaluable to create a mass, electoral-wing campaign that could achieve power by running candidates in elections who could then start implementing socialist policies in the government. In the face of these alternatives, others, such as Albert L. Couch, opined that electoral politics was a closed-off arena and suggested that the core of socialism was the expansion of the labor force along with holding strikes and the formation of own organizations as cooperatives and commune organizations.

The divergent ideas of the socialist strategy were, on the one hand, used to evoke favorable formations and, at times, confrontations in the socialist movement of Haverhill. In 1901, for instance, a meeting of dissidents was held, at which they proposed to secede from the SLP to become the Peoples Socialist Club, a direct-action group without elections. The division ultimately divided the SLP's voters in the elections and overstepping that division would aggravate tension in the years to come.

Their second source of internal division, this time an aspect of socialism in Haverhill, is the workers' concerned relations with other progressive and working-class organizations in the city. Socialists, a segment of the workers' and reformers' movements, have always felt themselves as occupants of this movement and have collaborated with such organizations as the AFL and WTUL to pursue their agenda. Nevertheless, these relationships were also often strained and bumpy as diverging interests led segments of the movement into political squabbling.

Socialism was a narrow pursuit. Therefore, the socialists had to compete among themselves to reach the council seats in the elections. Some socialists considered the unions as natural partners in the campaign against capitalism, but, on the other hand, Another group doubted the unions as they deemed them very pragmatic and caught up in the narrow bread-and-butter issues, not to mention their lack of total aspiration for the broad socialist vision. This came to its closest culmination over the infamous 'Shoe Strike of 1909', where some socialists felt that the unions settled off way too much for the manufacturers to the detriment of the workers.

The internal division and conflict among the Haverhill socialist movement had frequently been the means for disqualifying socialists, who were portrayed as disorganized, worthless, and even dangerous. Likewise, the Gazette even ran stories to lift the curtains on the conflicts and disagreements among the socialists, as the writers hoped the socialists would look like a divided group that was not trustworthy enough to give them the power to manage the city.

While the socialists were formulating how to achieve their goals on an equal footing with Haverhill's traditional power structures and politics, they had their backs against the wall. Nevertheless, they made progress through the ballot and the parliament, constantly running against the wall that was deeply rooted in the system so that it distributes wealth among the wealthy and helps the authorities.

One of the most obvious problems concerned the electoral system and the business and political classes declaring the winner. While the ward-shaped representation of Haverhill was gerrymandered and voter suppression limited, the socialists had a hard time winning seats in the council and other key bodies. Nevertheless, the chances were scarce, as the projected representatives from time to time won landslide elections yet found themselves flooded by the millions of financially powerful individuals who had control over offices and machines.

To tell the truth, contented socialist development in Haverhill was strongly impeded by the city's capitalist structure, in which limited corporations, wealthy family owners, and businessmen monopolized the entire economy and derived enormous benefits from the lives of the city's working-class people. Using strategies like municipal ownership and worker rights consciousness, socialists fought against the existence of the economic power center against strong opposition from wealthy businesspeople who used their clout to block legislation that would have impacted their establishment and authority. Such belief in their power and the meaning of their struggle encouraged them not to surrender and to try to overcome what seemed like an insurmountable obstacle.

A stunning showcase of such resilience and endeavor can be seen in the aftermath of the attack on the Haverhill Labor Temple in 1912 by the socialists. However, on the contrary, they became more daring and took the incident as a chance to get more supporters and draw their base. They mobilized the population on a large scale in the form of mass demonstrations and rallies to protest against the attack and seek justice for the victims. Through the coverage of the media directed by them, they were able to attract attention in society, which they then used to show the cruelty and corruption of their enemies.

The socialists then proved that they could not be caught by their opponents by making all the needed moves for power and advancing their agenda. They expanded their reach by running more candidates for office, organizing more strikes and protests, and trying to galvanize the working class to form their core support group. They extended their activism not only to their own Haverhill but also to allies and supporters beyond the town. This broadens their networks of solidarity with socialists and labor activists, both in the country and internationally.

The efforts exerted in this period had a good pay-off because, in subsequent years, the socialists gained more power and controlled more of the decision-making in the elections. In 1913, by electing three city council members, they gained significant control over the city's policies and the boundaries of future development. Amazingly enough, they reached that goal in 1915, when they almost accomplished what would have been impossible just years ago: electing one of their mayors.

However, the Haverhill Socialists were formidable to adverse conditions as well as different types of adversaries. Their struggle and enterprise to make a society follow the ideal remain the same. Despite the violence, repression, and obstacles, they ceased to get organized, agitate, and build power by mandating their dreams and drawing their strength from the rest of the city's working class.

The socialist's strength and the resilience of this plan were muscles that could, in one sense, be stretched and shaped to meet unexpected situations and learn from new challenges in the process. As an illustration, during their time, the socialists, faced with ideological differences among their allies, did everything possible to find a point where they could unite and concentrate efforts on common goals and values. When all the range of equal authority was against business and political elites, they approached it differently and tacitly maneuvered.

Socialists got acceptance from their working-class neighborhoods, and this was a key factor in their resilience, being the source of their endurance. Later, this led to a sense of mission and purpose, which took them to the end of the world. The socialists weren't just like any brick-and-mortar parties or a cluster of abstract thoughts; they were in the living, beating hearts of neighborhoods, workplaces, and institutions in Haverhill. With its base in lower classes and workers, the socialists' dedication to democracy and empowerment of communities provided them with what was otherwise lacking from their competitors. They had the staying power and legitimacy that nobody could have hoped to match.

To put it simply, it was their inextinguishable conviction that the cause they were fighting for was both right and worthy of victory that kept them determined to the end. Even in the grave hours, when forces of reaction seemed to be coming up and closing out from all directions, socialist groups remained assured that they had been on the right side of history and victory would not be far-fetched.

This belief in the superiority of their ideals and the potency of their actions gave them the pluck that they required to soldier on, despite the seeming discouraging odds against their campaign.

Another strong example here is the resilience and stand of socialists against such an act in 1912 during the bombing of the Haverhill Labor Temple. Contrary to the cowardice and submissiveness portrayed by the antagonists, the socialists used the incident as a launching point to thrive and gather support. They organized the biggest-ever marches and rallies to protest the attack and to act as the voice of the victims in demanding justice. To that end, they used to air the incident to the general public as a means to disclose the brutality and the grief of their enemies.

While socialists recovered from the shock of the attack even more determinedly, that did not mean they were brutally engaged and did not feel themselves to be the leaders in this struggle. They competed electorally by nominating more candidates for office, mobilizing more strikes and protests, and aiming to get backing from working-class residents of the city. They also sought help from allies and sympathizers who lived beyond Haverhill. They just formed a social network within the global labor movement and socialist circles.

Such attempts in the forthcoming years indeed reaped the coveted fruits when the socialist party largely gained votes and increased its influence at high decision-making levels. In 1913, they supported three candidates for the city council and, as a result, had enough to control the city's politics, which affected the planning of the city's plan. In 1515, they were almost elected the mayor of the city, which can be compared to a meager possibility several years ago.

Naturally, the socialist triumphs could never be total or unopposed either. Hence, they always encountered opposition, and they also met with many setbacks in their endeavor. However, their contention for social justice in their neighborhood lit the flame of socialism in Haverhill, which was strengthening as a big socialist movement in the United States was losing momentum after World War I.

CHAPTER 6

The Legacy Of Haverhill Socialism In Labor Movements

The socialist movement in Haverhill, Massachusetts, which took root in the first half of the 20th century, is one of the striking events that shaped the social life of the town and the whole of American labor politics. For this, the socialists of Haverhill can be thanked for much of the labor movement of their time and even up to now. Through their sophisticated organizing, the unbreakable obligation to workers' rights, and the economic justice system, their big dream of a more democratic and better society helped to shape the labor movement, especially at that time.

This chapter is about how socialism in Haverhill has influenced and is still surviving concerning workplace issues and trade unions. The course will consider socialist elements in these movements, including the major efforts of the mill workers (textile strikes in the early 1900s) leading to the acceptance of industrial unionism in 1930 and later times. Yet this history shows us the role of solidarity and collective action during challenging times, such as economic exploitation and unsafe working conditions. Still, those principles have been the keepers and spirits of the few who sacrificed themselves in the ongoing labor actions of our time. The discussion can focus on the broader importance of a vision and example of the socialist comrades of Haverhill for the laboring community's ongoing struggle for workers' rights and economic democracy in the US as well as in the world.

From the beginning of the occupation of the socialist movement in Haverhill, which happened in the early years of the city, the links between the movement and the workers' struggles can be seen. Many of the leaders of the movement, along with James Carey, Albert Couch, and Martha Moore Avery, who were also among those people who had worked in Haverhill's factories and mills, had a chance to fully recognize the conditions of hard work, low wages, and being stripped of fundamental rights and protections that had dominated the industrial labor of the early 20th century.

These encounters, along with the ideas of socialist ideology and their beliefs about building up an egalitarian society, convinced most people of socialist leanings, and they took an active involvement in the city's labor movement. What they considered the main strategy was the organization of workers and their ability to fight against the powerful class of capitalists, which was a real problem for ordinary workers trying to make ends meet in those hard times.

One of the first and most effective events of this cooperation with socialists and workers was the quality season strike of 1899. The strike, which lasted more than a week, had thousands of textile workers from the several mills and factories in the city demanding compensation for the various pay cuts, decrees, and layoffs issued by the textile manufacturers in the aftermath of a recession. The workers, which were the youthful women and immigrants too, called for the restoration of their wages, compensation, and previous working situations and recognized that they had the right to unionize and bargain.

The care of working men and women in Haverhill was the main activity of the socialists. They gave some monetary assistance and arranged the strike. They not only created strike committees and relief funds and used their political weight to influence local officials and business leaders to achieve the workers' demands, but they also drew up and distributed leaflets, held public speeches, and organized demonstrations and mass assemblies. Besides, they made efforts to fight ethnic and linguistic segregation. They concluded that it was unity and common action that could secure this strike.

The workers, despite the manufacturers and their supporters in the police and the government, would not possibly relent. Consequently, they would eventually triumph, with their key demands restored and thus their right to unionize recognized. The win was a landmark in the labor movement in Haverhill and gave the city a central position of flourishing working cohesion and empathy.

In the latter years, Haverhill's followers of socialism were the chief figureheads for the city's movement that addressed the labor problem. They played a major role in developing and promoting general strikes and riots across the textile, footwear, and transportation industries. They combined their efforts towards creating a union of trade workers and their unions. They went beyond their shop floors and used their powers to influence policies like establishing a minimum wage and the problems of child labor.

The main contribution assigned to the socialist involvement in the Haverhill labor movement was their campaign for democracy from the bottom ranks and worker control. Another characteristic that was missing in those other socialist organizations was the ability to allow the workers' participation and decision-making in the activity, which then became a characteristic that flourished within the SLP of Haverhill and later the lodges of the AFL affiliates in the city.

This element of local democracy was embodied in the design and implementation of the Haverhill Labor Union. Unions and other worker bodies commonly had striking committees composed of rank-and-file members but not by leaders appointed from an outside institution or another source. During meetings, we formed our opinions, also welcoming differing views to the table and keeping the entire token holders updated with all the crucial decisions being made. As a result, stoppages and other types of labor were initiated and led by the workers themselves and not consistently by the union leaders from above.

The leadership of these people made sure that control and democracy in the workplace were key, since this generated ownership and investment among the Haverhill working class. It augmented the solidarity and impregnability of a pro-worker community, which incorporated the basic communist manifesto of a system where the masses can directly determine the outcomes that are favorable to them individually and as a whole.

Another vital legacy of socialists' ventures into labor, like in Haverhill, was the single status they upheld for the movement, which should be multilevel, inclusive, and intersectional to be able to unite workers of different industries, occupations, and social identities. The American labor movement in the early period was often split based on race, ethnicity, gender, and skill level. However, combating these detachments and building a unified and more powerful working class was the mission of the Haverhill socialists.

Built on these fundamentals of the Haverhill socialists was their strive for inclusion and unity, which they also reflected in their organizing and supporting workers in the fields of the textile and shoe industries, among nurses, physicians, and domestic workers. They also attempted to connect these labor movements with the pool of progressive and reform struggles of the women's suffragettes and the civil rights movements, realizing that the strife of the workers was not independent of broader social and economic equation movements.

The Union socialists put forward the idea of waged workers as a large, cross-cutting mainstream of a labor movement, which reflects the debates and struggles that have been defining the American labor movement in the decades ahead. It did not just mark the beginning of labor unions; it was, at that time, the precursor of the industrial unionism of the 1930s and the years after, the stage on which most American labor politics were performed, and it brought spectacular and historic workers' gains.

Engraved in the souls of the Haverhill socialists was an attitude of oneness, like rallying and unifying workers. They knew that it was the united action of the workers—their ability to negotiate together for better working conditions and higher pay—that made them strong. Thus, they refused to accept the tyranny of working in unsafe conditions and to be deprived of obtaining higher wages.

This devotion to solidarity was anchored in an all-encompassing socialist analysis of how wasteful the system of capitalism is and how, in the end, the poor and the working class are oppressed and exploited to the benefit of the select rich on top. Haverhill socialists were aware that laborers and capitalists had a conflict of interest. They also had the obvious opinion that the only way the workers could get better wages, working conditions, and living standards was by unionizing or joining a trade union.

Another very effective instance of this solidarity in action during these times was the 1912 textile strike ("Bread and Roses"), which was also known as the "Great Strike.". The strike, which started in Lawrence, Massachusetts, and later gained momentum across the towns in the whole of New England, especially the textile centers of Haverhill, was and was protested diluted wages and speed-ups initiated by the textile industry owners after a new state law reducing the maximum workweek of women and children.

A major part of the strikers were the immigrants, mainly the women and the children, who were confronted by very cruel repression from the police or the private security forces of the manufacturers. However, they faced countermovement on the other side too when the army and police were deployed to end the strike while most workers and activists in the country sided with their cause to walk out, many of whom were socialists from Haverhill traveled to Lawrence to join the picket line and provide material aid and moral support to the workers on strike.

The Lawrence movement is still considered a pivotal event in U.S. labor history. Launching the presidential election campaign, it divided the workers and activists into two groups involving labor unionism and voter solidarity. Not only did it drastically affect the harming labor movement in Haverhill, but many organized strikes were held after the demonstration, which became more rebellious after the strike.

These communist socialists were keen on showing solidarity and creating worker power as essential strategies for achieving fairness for the working folks. They contributed to the coordination and participation of a whole range of strikes and protests in various sectors and workplaces: shoe factories, streetcar shops, and service industries.

Part of this imagery, signifying the importance of the movement, was the great shoe strike of 1918–1919, in which thousands of workers in Haverhill shoe factories participated. The strike, which took place immediately after the shoe manufacturers had reduced wages and sacked workers, aimed to address the menace of toxic working conditions that plagued several of the plant factories in the city.

The strikers received intense opposition not only from the manufacturers but also from the state and police, who used different means like arrest and violence to break down their strike, causing the workers to not fully organize. However, they also had a vote of confidence from the Haverhill socialists and other activist organizations, which created committees to organize the strike, raise funds for the strikers as well as their families, and finally build an attachment in the people for the workers' demands.

But through their efforts, despite the arising problems and failures, the shoemakers of Haverhill eventually realized they had better pay and working conditions, as well as much more power at their workplace, hence the teams and the grievance processes. The victory was proof of the might of unity, cooperation, and a strong bond between the socialists of Haverhill and the working class. This continues to contribute to the characterization of the latter as the true representatives of the workers.

Besides the social arena, which was crucial for the Hill socialists in building solidarity and a collective approach, there was the struggle for well-paying jobs with no injuries. Similar to many industrial cities of that period, Haverhill was plagued by a myriad of occupational hazards and diseases, including the crushing scarring of lungs with the dust of the textile mills and the abomination of poisonous fumes and chemicals of the shoe factories.

The socialists of Haverhill realized that the causes of these accidents were not only the carelessness of one or other individuals or a matter of just bad luck but that they were capitalism, part of the system and the roots of industrial capitalism, placing money over men. They asserted that the only way to create a decent and secure work environment is by establishing stringent regulations, a tightly enforced system, and empowerment and control by the laborers themselves.

This effort, which they championed through the establishment of and support of campaigns and efforts to elevate workplace safety and healthiness, was one of their critical roles. They worked tirelessly to get through the provisions of state and local laws for safety inspection, ventilation requirements, and other safety measures in factories and mills. These leaders were leaders by example. They set an example through their actions. Through publications, meetings, and demonstrations, the workers were mobilized and educated about these issues.

The seriousness of the impact on workers' health from the mills prompted Haverhill to open its Occupational Disease Clinic in 1919. The clinic operates during the workers' free time, with the staff being rotational part-timers. This method is carried out through donations from workers as well as the organizations related to them. It renders medical servicing as well as hold of workers who are offended by some illnesses or cultivated injuries over work.

Right away, the clinic was the first ever socialist healthcare facility in the Haverhill area, which served as a representative of the belief that the socialists held about their duty to mutual aid as well as solidarity. In such a way, it was possible, and it also increased social awareness and concern about the condition of workers who had been affected by industrial dangers to their health and well-being. Shaping the ancient reform movement in the United States for workers' benefits and safety was also a part of its considerable influence.

What the Haverhill socialists especially stand out for is the fact that, unlike previous unions, they are founded on the principles of solidarity and collective action as a response to capital exploitation and unsafe working conditions. It is without a doubt that the socialist way of thinking had an impressive and phenomenal influence on the American labor movement. This contributed to the workers' union's strong union campaigns, such as the large strikes of the 1930s and the health and safety occupational campaigns started in the 1960s and 1970s.

It also acted as a cultural definer of the labor movement's ethos and ideals, such as occupational campaigns for mutual aid, which workers began seeing as crucial aspects of their struggle for proper pay and respect. There should be unions in the trade and more picket lines, songs, and strike slogans that enumerate the spirit of solidarity and that all in the Haverhill socialists communicate to the present existence and are progressing during the struggles of working people.

The vision of the Haverhill socialists in American labor history mobilizes much more than the direct work they did as organizers and advocates in the 19th century. They were a guide in so many fields of formation and support of the labor movement, not only in terms of creating ideological and strategic principles of the movement but also leaving behind themselves a set of core socialist principles and values of humanism that permeate the daily lives of workers and the community. other

The core of this idea of socialism was a strong belief in human dignity and rights, and this included workers of all backgrounds and professions. Demonstrating this socialist stance, Haverhill socialists firmly denied the existence of a certain group of workers who were more valuable or deserving of money than other workers and who were more valuable or deserving of money than other workers and difficulties among all

The dedication and solidarity among workers, as well as status equality, were the Haverhill socialists' means of building a diversified and inclusive labor movement so that it could help workers regardless of the industry, their profession, or other social identities. They chose to organize and support those workers who were not likely members of a union due to inequality and discrimination, mostly women, immigrants, and African Americans.

In 1903, the year when a group of dedicated women from Haverhill formed the Woman's Trade Union League as part of the SLP, the organization became the first in the United States to focus on the unique needs and problems of women who worked for low wages in manufacturing industries. The League gave women an environment where they could meet and exchange their womanhood experiences, know what to do next and develop the courage to demand better working conditions and be provided with a wide range of rights and protections.

Also, the Haverhill socialists played the role of the earliest and very vigorously advocated for the rights of immigrant workers, who, most of the time, had to endure injustices without any support. They promoted strikes and demonstrations that were performed by immigrants and aimed to unite and support them. They played a primary role in socializing and encoding among the workers of different linguistic and ethnic groups.

Such a willingness of the workers to stand together, whether in principle or simply for the sake of the survival of the labor movement, was not just a moral or ethical position but a strongly vital strategy. The Haverhill socialists understood these differences could be effectively overcome by organizing and consolidating as an organized body with power commensurate with their numbers. Therefore, the exclusiveness or stratification of the working class that contributes to the degradation and erosion of all working people's power will hamper their role as a powerful group.

FC (Another key socialist principle that this town helped bring into the world of work was a critique of capitalism and a vision of a much fairer and more equitable system to replace it.). The people who make up the Haverhill socialists chose to adopt the ideology that capitalism was neither natural nor evitable and that it was a construct, one that was created with the sole purpose of maintaining the hold of the very few to everyone's disadvantage.

They asserted that such ills as poverty, inequality, and worker exploitation are not due to an individual's incapability or failure to try hard. Rather, they are due to the systemic capitalist underpinnings of the system. As they thought, the workers could be liberated from their unhealthy economic conditions to be able to prosper only when the system was challenged and eventually replaced by a new economic order founded upon public ownership, democracy, and equity for all.

This socialist idea of capitalism critically influenced the American labor movement, and therefore, if that movement was molded along such political and ideological directions, characterization. Though unions and the labor movement as a whole did not explicitly strive for socialism, many of their members began to perceive their role as partly fighting for the workers' rights and economic justice that inherently strive against the capitalist elite's power and privileges.

This anti-capitalist characterization of the labor struggle movement was not just seen in the demands and strategies of several of the major battles that took place in the 20th century but in those as well, such as sit-down strikes in the 1930s and public sector unionization in the 1960s and 1970s. Along with it, it spurred on the birth of a new generation of labor leaders and activists who thought they were dealing with a single issue, e.g., poor economic status or unemployment, and, at the same time, social and political change.

The socialists of Haverhill adhered to masterless democracy and worker empowerment, two ideas that strongly and irreversibly influenced the way people thought about labor. They thought that workers were the main source of the greatness of the countries and the movement, rather than the mere voice of the union bosses or the outside leaders.

Such was the grassroots vocation of those who pursued trade unions and continued in leadership, such as CIO industrial unions and the 21st century-based community workers' centers. These organizations strived for the involvement of employees in the decision-making process and aimed at overcoming the workers' passivity by creating a feeling of solidarity around the common goal.

Education as a concept and aesthetic development, as stressed by the Haverhill socialists, was yet another significant principle that left an impact on the views of the workers as a whole. They were convinced that there couldn't be a division between the struggle of the workers for their economic justice and political liberation, on the one hand, and the struggle for cultural and intellectual freedom, on the other. What will be a real liberation for labor is also everyone's right to take part in maximum human development.

This principle is demonstrated in the different cultural and educational programs that the associates of Haverhill socialists and her companions helped to conduct, starting from labor colleges to workers' theaters and choral associations. During these schemes, comrades and workers could meet up, communicate their problems, and show respect for each other as comrades, which contributed to the sense of identity and belonging of the movement.

Haverhill Shoe Factory Workers

CHAPTER 7

Haverhill Socialism's Impact On Civil Rights And Social Justice

The socialism that was embraced fervently in Haverhill, Massachusetts, in the early decades of the 20th century was, in essence, a fight for economic justice and workers' liberties. However, along with rising and growing, the movement began to learn that the struggle for socialism was impossible, apart from other issues including civil rights and social justice. The socialists in Haverhill were aware that the same systems of power and oppression that threw the backs of the workers into the chains of prejudice and starvation also confined and dehumanized women, people of color, immigrants, and other excluded or deprived groups. In light of this, they were of the view that socialism embraces the fight against discrimination and sexism, among other vices, as a basic part of their concept.

In this chapter, the socialist movement in Haverhill will be studied to witness proof of the intertwining social justice and civil rights struggle that it contributed to. We will consider the activities of socialist leaders and activists who are concerned with selling, buying, and creating/eliminating various forms of discrimination and oppression, both within the movement itself and outside. We will talk about how the socialists' wish for intersectionality and the majority's harmony through differences of various sorts made them progressives both at their time and in the future. Finally, in our consideration of Haverhill socialism, we will highlight the wide impact of that socialism on the outcome of social equality and even political equality in the United States and other parts of the world.

The term intersectionality, which stands for the fact that different types of oppression and inequality are mutually reinforcing and that different forms of oppression can't be properly grasped if explored separately, often refers to the feminist and anti-racist movements of the late 20th century. On the other hand, the socialist movement of Haverhill greatly preceded this idea by realizing how classes, races, genders, and other identity configurations and social levels were not only overlapping but also deeply intertwined.

Initially, the socialists of Haverhill knew that the quest for economic fairness was not an independent branch of the social and political equity revolt. Utilizing the same capitalist system that was responsible for the exploitation and impoverishment of workers, they also realized the injustices and prejudice it has caused in the development of racism, sexism, xenophobia, and other bigotry and oppression that have been bred over time. They argued that the ruling classes mainly took advantage of the divisions among the workers and grew powerful with a working class that remained fragmented along the lines of race, gender, ethnicity, and nationality. This solidarity could only be maintained when the working class challenged the power of capital.

This intersectional approach, which is the order of the day for many socialist speakers and writers in the city, reflects this aspect. Couch, an activist on the Haverhill societal platform, observed in a 1903 article in "The Comrade," a socialist journal, that "the Negro question is not a question of race but of class." He noted with emphasis that the black workers in Haverhill and here and there were prone to the same exploitation and bigotry in conditions as the white workers and that uniting over the capitalist system did not discriminate based on color and had no concept of division by color. ' He notes that it uses the so-called slavery of the Black and tells the white worker that it keeps him also in the dark by using his prejudice against the different races.'

Socialist women in Haverhill also recognized that the issues of class were rooted in the very essence of gender inequality. They contended that women workers not merely faced exploitation, but it was a dual of workers and women, meaning that women's cause was equal if not more important than the general struggle of socialism. In 1912, Jessie Ashley, an activist, said, "The question of women's rights and labor issues cannot be separated." She did so while noting that a large portion of industrial workers were women, and they were frequently paid less than men for the same tasks and were not allowed to join many benefits unions provided. The emancipation of the working class and women should be done simultaneously, "she declared.

The socialists, with different identities within Haverhill, saw how immigration and xenophobia were designed to keep the poor class apart simultaneously. In contrast to many industrial cities that were built at the beginning of the 20th century with ethnic immigrants making a great deal of the population, Haverhill had a large and polygenic immigrant population, such as people from Ireland, Italy and Poland. What differentiated the socialists from their local and workers' ideas of nativism and xenophobia was their willingness to have a universal work-class unity that transcended nationality.

In 1912, the socialist movement in Haverhill developed a stronghold when William J. Bohn, the editor of The Clarion, a local socialist paper, argued in an editorial that only the Socialist Party stood for the rights of the foreign-born workers. He confirmed the discrimination, exploitation, and abuse of immigrant workers from Haverhill to anywhere else and that the socialist movement had a "the stranger must not be considered our enemy," his writings say. He is "our fellow adventurer in the world of the international working class."

This was also seen in the internationalist politics and antiracism promoted by Haverhill socialists in their form of organization and operation. They actively brought in and supported the immigrant workers, released their materials in multiple languages, and helped to establish some joint files between the ethnic and national groups falling inside the working class of the town. At the same time, they made political ties with socialist forces and labor movements in other countries; thus, the Okinawans looked at their fight against capitalism and imperialism as a sort of global strike.

The socialists in Haverhill at times indeed managed to stand out as an example of inclusivity and cooperation, but they did not always succeed in being true to that model. Being a movement of this sort, it was undoubtedly influenced by the prejudices and shortcomings of the time. While some socialist groups or leaders did espouse racist or intolerable views in the early days of the movement, these prejudiced ideas usually remained without being properly challenged, and relevant challenges, like those faced by women, immigrants, and people of color, were not prioritized. During the movement, it was verified that the classes were involved in their politics, and hence the movement differentiated between classes and other forms of oppression.

However, they were prompted by the hindrances and undermined by the socialists in Haverhill, who differentiated between a movement that was transformative in such a way. Through their communication, they came to realize that the fight for socialism went beyond economic justice into a society where everyone could live on an equal footing that was not determined by race, gender, ethnicity, or nationality. Moreover, these individuals understood that bringing about this change could only be won through a fight against the entire economic system, including all those intricate systems that were in place and were fueling it.

The socialist movement in Haverhill did not just enunciate in theory the idea that intersectionality and solidarity needed to be the basis. It is worth mentioning that it did not only theoretically confront but also practically act against numerous types of social inequalities and discrimination within the movement and society at large.

The struggle against racial discrimination and segregation was among the most critical concerns for the socialists who were supporting the town of Haverhill. Just as with the many cities in the North, segregation by law in the early 1900s was surprisingly absent at Haverhill during that period. But despite that, there were still barriers and fences that were used to keep black people outside, and this continued the oppression. Black people mostly worked at the most prosaic and risky jobs that could not offer them proper financial stability, and they had to deal with prejudice and outrageousness from white civilians and structures.

The socialists in Haverhill realized they were facing this racial injustice as a manifestation of direct opposition to working-class unity and socialist solutions. According to them, oppression was a manipulation of the ruling class to create better competition and divisions among the workers and keep them from the people who oppressed the working classes. Whereas many antiracists envisioned a post-racial society based on the liberation objective and equality of all peoples, others focused on the need to confront racism and discrimination at a more local level, within the socialist movement and the community at large.

This was their objective, and they achieved this by deporting and sponsoring the membership of black The socialists of this city also showed their willingness to back and strengthen the black activists and organizations in Haverhill. In 1910, the socialists, who were the primary actors in the Haverhill Central Labor Union, gave money to the local chapter of the National Association of Colored People (NAACP). Socialist workers also teamed up with the Niagara Movement, which was a civil rights movement for blacks founded by W.E.B. Du Bois in 1905. They were instrumental to the organization's endeavor to overcome racial disadvantage caused by apartheid in the whole state and beyond as well.

Lastly, socialists did not limit their work on this issue to an emotional connection with the sufferers. Instead, they used their political influence to push for real changes and reforms that would most likely address racial inequality in Haverhill. In 1913, socialist city councilor James F. Careens stood up for the local black people's rights by introducing a resolution that condemned the city's policy of segregating black and white prisoners in the local jail. The resolution was incorporated and helped raise awareness about the real problem of racial discrimination in the criminal justice system.

The socialists fought for the elimination of real estate differentiation and segregation in Haverhill as well. They backed a successful campaign by voters to integrate the city's public housing, all of which had been segregated until that time. In 1915, John C. Chase, a mayor with socialist leanings, appointed a black man, William H. Lewis, to the Boston Board of Assessors. Lewis thus became one of the first black people ever to hold any major public office in the state of Massachusetts.

Mayor John C. Chase 1898-1900

The socialist revolutionaries worked even harder, beyond political discrimination, for this group of people. They did not only build the perception of racial unity and acknowledgment among the working-class communities but also united them.

Socialist union workers not only created interracial gatherings to unite blacks and whites and organized social activities like dances, picnics, and theater presentations but also broke racial borders.

people who were within the socialist movement. Back in 1902, at one of the meetings of the Haverhill Socialist Labor Party, Thomas H.H. Walker, the black socialist from Boston, was chosen as a guest. Walker's presence served as a powerful symbol of both socialists intent to ensure a fair society regarding racial issues and to strive for equality and unity with the other white socialists which eventually resulted in changing some of the socialist members' way of thinking on racial matters. Apart from this, they pushed for white workers to lend support to the efforts and campaigns of black workers, who became natural allies, because they knew these struggles were part of a broader war against discrimination and class exploitation.

It was the quest of the socialists of Haverhill towards fighting for equal opportunities and women's rights that signaled the end game for the political parties. The previous parts of the article show that socialist women from Haverhill regarded gender suppression as intrinsically connected with class exploitation; they chose all their efforts to advance women's liberation within the socialist movement and in the community at large.

They achieved it mainly by leading the campaign for the suffrage of women and giving women a political voice. The State Woman Suffrage Association, which was founded in Haverhill in 1870, had links with the socialist movement, and some women even joined the campaign for women's suffrage. B Leveraging public art as a form of deliberation can enhance community well-being in several ways. In 1915, the Haverhill Socialist Party included the "Massachusetts Suffrage Referendum" on their election calendar. This would have led to women getting the right to vote in all state elections. Despite failing to win voting rights for female citizens, this referendum did give a stimulus to the democratic struggle and listed the seventeenth amendment, which was introduced in the constitution in 1920 in a historical age.

The Haverhill socialist women's efforts were aimed at not only tackling gender discrimination and inequalities that existed in the workplace but also, at the same time, challenging the patriarchal system that controlled society then. They lobbied to earn equal wages for work done and to eradicate the abusive conditions women in the factories and mills of the city had to face. In the summer of 1912, socialist activist Glendower Evans worked as an organizer who won the strike of Haverhill textile women, who empowered the cause of better payment conditions. The strike that had been going on for weeks was a strong symbol of the great power that solidarity and collective action among women possessed. These examples later sparked similar actions in other cities.

Furthermore, the women of socialism involved themselves with diverse feminist causes through the manifold reform movements. They sparred for the control of contraception and reproductive rights, and they won that battle because they saw these things as crucial to women's health, and they also enjoyed the autonomy of the women. They advocated to eliminate domestic violence and sexual harassment and to provide assistance to the survivors of such abuses. The role women played in their community cannot be overstated. They gave more weight to the issue of the representation of women in politics and public service and addressed this fact by arguing that the highest form of democracy requires women to be completely involved, both as leaders and followers.

One of the most notable socialist women in Haverhill was Martha Moore Avery, a schoolteacher who was one among the young socialists in the early 20th century and ignited a socialist movement in the city Avery was an avid and active proponent of female rights as well as equality of genders, and she used her status as a leader in the socialistic movement to move these issues forward. As the election got closer, she spoke during a speech in 1908, stating that "Socialism is the only hope for working women." To her, inequality prevention and women's liberation were crucial to the accomplishment of workers' social and economic goals.

Avery and other women supporters in Haverhill also tried to establish the places and providers that provided a voice for women and developed their ability to lead and struggle. By 1903, for example, Avery had helped bring the socialist women of Haverhill into one club, which was a base for the women to discuss politics, navigate the campaigns, and create a force that supported and empathized with women's empowerment and leadership the purposes of the club, and it has done an excellent job of evolving the women's movement in Haverhill and beyond.

Furthermore, the struggles of social activists in Haverhill included much more than getting rid of racial and gender inequality. Hence, they developed a supportive community and advocated against other forms of discrimination and marginalization. A special preference of the socialists was the immigrants' rights and ethnic minorities, whom the socialists saw as a part of the broader labor class and would not give in to typical American socialists' nativism and xenophobia. Even more importantly, they were the first groups fighting for the individual human rights of people with disabilities, including accessibility and inclusion of the disabled in public institutions and places.

The most perfect instance of the socialists' egalitarianism and solidarity by standing on the opposite of commercial and multiple types of discrimination against sometimes the most disadvantaged groups is the socialists' support for the Industrial Workers of the World (IWW). The IWW was striving for a maximalist labor organizing strategy that included all workers, regardless of color, nationality, specific skill, or sex. In 1905, the International Workers of the World was born in this city, and its members were active in the movement around socialism. They were in partnership with this city's socialist movement. Unlike most organized labor unions during that period, where leaders were not actively involved, the Industrial Workers of the World didn't have leaders who weren't active members of the union. People involved in the Women's Trade Union League (WTUL) knew that this entity was the most important tool for creating a more equal and protest-based workers' movement.

The attempt by socialists in Haverhill to replace racial discrimination, gender prejudice, and a series of oppressions had an important effect on the city itself and the wide landscape of American politics and society in the early 20th century.

Many of the socialist workers in Haverhill were leaders and forerunners of the Progressive Era, a time of important political and social reform intended to reprimand the evils, shortcomings, and injustices of industrial capitalism. The Socialists' unwavering advocacy for economic freedom, political democracy, and the elimination of social inequalities propelled many demands and struggles that became the progressive movements' cause. This was comprised of women's suffrage, labor rights, efforts to abolish corruption, and the resetting of monopolistic power.

The socialists in the Haverhill community did not merely surpass their working-class brethren in the way that many of the Progressives did; they also used an intersectional approach to social justice and political reform. Although a few of the progressives concentrated their strives for social adjustment by fighting on the part of particular subjects, the socialists were cognizant that these patterns of oppression and inequalities were not just separate but also mutually beneficial, and the attainment of true liberty would be affected by a tremendously comprehensive and systemic reformation of society.

In this view, the Haverhill socialists were the precursors to the concept referred to as "identity politics," which asserts that struggles have to be built upon the different experiences and needs of an oppressed group, and solidarity should not be only a matter of an oppressor-oppressed dichotomy. The civil rights movement built on this strategy and this line of struggle would be carried on by the feminist movement, the LGBTQ+ movement, and other liberation struggles in the following decades.

The Haverhill socialists not only helped the willingness of the American left community and made contributions to the creation of the American left but also strengthened the roots of left-wing politics in the United States. On the other hand, although the Socialist Party of America came to be a derivative of the Socialist Labor Party declining in 1901, it will never be in a limelight position as, like its European profiles, it still played a crucial role in the formation of the political and intellectual landscape of the early 20th century. A number of the chief inspirational people within the American left circle, like Eugene V. Debs and Norman Thomas, together with Emma Goldman and W.E.B. Du Bois, were greatly motivated and excited by the teachings and principles of the Haverhill of the New Hampshire socialists as well.

Additionally, their impact on the socialist figure on the American left was also equally huge. They also exerted their influence on the wider labor movement. As mentioned, the socialists were deeply involved in industrial unionism, and their movement was in line with the IWW and other extreme labor organizations. They were leading the way in formulating fresh approaches to the labor movement in all sectors and occupations. They have been at the center of almost all the labor disputes of the early twentieth century, none of which is the Lawrence Textile Strike of 1912 and so on.

Socialist dedication to industrial unionism and working-class harmony was also a significant revolution in the American labor movement on a larger scale. Though the IWW lapsed eventually due to the iron dictatorship, it was in the armed surroundings of inter-spirit competition and inner division that other groups took up and transformed its spirit into that of a militant and all-inclusive movement of the working masses. The Industrial Organizations that arose in the 1930s as an enemy that was more conservative than the AFL (the American Federation of Labor) were heavily influenced by the experience and theories of the IWW and other socialist-affiliated unions.

Socialists' Triumph in Haverhill
The Boston Daily Globe

CHAPTER 8

Cultural and artistic expressions of Haverhill Socialism

The socialist boon that reigned in Haverhill, Massachusetts, in the 20th century was not only a political, economic, and cultural phenomenon. They used a variety of storytelling tools, like literature and journalism, as well as performing arts such as visual arts and performing arts, to provide space to enlighten and inspire the masses and shape the cultural environment of Haverhill to look the way they wished. In this chapter, we delve deep into the artistic imprints of Haverhill socialism by considering the extent to which its values, aspirations, and struggles were reflected in this artwork.

The ability of art and culture to educate, agitate, and inspire those in Haverhill was readily appreciated by the socialist movement there. They discovered art and literature not as a way to relax or to obtain something private but as a medium to have an impact and to bring about change. This implied that the top APF leadership not only promoted the production and spread of artistic and cultural socialist matters but also extended such promotion beyond the movement into the whole community.

A big way in which socialists went about implementing art and literature as propaganda vehicles was by publishing socialist newspapers, magazines, and pamphlets. The Haverhill Socialist, a weekly newspaper between 1898 and 1921, was the key opposition voice during that time and thus was an influential factor in most political dissertations. The paper, under the leadership of Albert L. Couch and afterward by James F. Carey, became a key destination where socialist ideas, news, and analysis were reported. It reached about 9,000 readers per week.

The Haverhill Socialist had a wide range of content, and the mix included local, national, and international news, commentaries, theories, and cultural content. It centered on each of these social concerns of the moment, which ranged from labor strikes and electoral battles to women's liberation and anti-imperialism. At the same time, I, too, was exposed to various forms of art, ranging from poems to short stories, reviews of literature, and other content that had socialist themes.

The Socialist Sunday School column, one of the sections of the newspaper regularly, presented socialist ideas and principles simply and quickly for the use of children and young people. The writing included stories, fables, and parables enhanced with messages of cohesion, equality, and social justice. In this way, it is intended to encourage young readers to open their minds about the real world.

In addition to prose that was reflective of their political stance, they also published original poetry and fiction by local writers. A great part of this literature depicted social problems, addressed labor concerns, and depicted a socialist utopia. To illustrate, a 1901 version of the paper has a poem titled "The Coming Day" by Mary Fletcher, in which it prophesizes a socialist future where "all shall share the wealth they make" and "none shall suffer for the greedy gain." Another one of them, "The Toiler's Song" by John Macbeth, celebrates the dignity and power of labor and minim

Moreover, these socialists in Haverhill did not rely on the socialist newspaper only to advocate for their cause. They also produced more than one type of publication that used art and literature to promote their message. The Comrade, the monthly publication of the Haverhill Socialist Club, contained original literary works such as essays, poems, and stories, as well as artwork expressing socialist themes, both local pieces and from nationally known socialist writers. The Clarion was a brief socialist paper from 1902 that had a page with book reviews, cultural articles, and original works of art under the "Literary Section" on schedule.

In the same vein, performances and cultural events also became key for the socialists to communicate their vision and further the cohesion within their movement. The Haverhill Socialist Club set its focus on socialist education activities in the form of lectures, debates, concerts, and theatrical works where political matters were treated along with entertainment. One of the known events was "Socialist Vaudeville," a variety show that featured skits, songs, and sketches that parodied excess capitalism and socialist values.

The socialists from Haverhill also organized cultural activities and events that aimed at surveying, planting, and instilling socialist values and ideas early in life. Socialist Sunday School, which was open from 1900 until 1905, held classes on socialist history, ideology, and beliefs much like in other schools, using songs, stories, and different games. Besides the organizing of socialistic-themed pageants, picnics, and other events that ensured the socialist family's involvement and also ensured the feeling of community and shared purpose,

The causes of the socialists in Haverhill were not limited to this programming and institutions of involvement but also permeated their day-to-day lives and social events with a socialist culture and ethics. They held fellowship picnics and parties in the halls of the factory to the socialist pledges and clung to the songs and socialist poetry in rallies and demonstrations. They decorated their homes and workplaces with pictures and words of socialist images. Indeed, for so many socialists, their devotion to socialism was also a kind that embraced themselves, including both public and private life.

Strangely enough, the acts of art and culture linked with Haverhill socialism were not deemed a way of only encouraging socialism in the abstract sense, but they gave meaning to the specific predicament and adversity of the local people and community. It is often the artworks that reflect not only these groups but also their neighborhood(s), likes, challenges, and aspirations that were shared by all at that time. They provided a socialist point of view on how inequality and social problems should be addressed. The resisting groups also offered an alternative means to achieve social harmony.

One of the crucial topics that one of the most Haverhill socialist artists and writers covered was the exploitation and oppression of labor under Capitalism. Socialists got a clear view of how the working class in the city's factories, mills, and workshops was being treated when they saw that they lacked the fundamental necessities of life influenced by the social and economic system. Through their bewitching art forms, they were the vigor house of fiery protests that raged against the decadence of society.

As an illustration, articles, and columns of The Haverhill Socialist would often expose the ghastly realities of the wage slave's life in the city, where the workers endured crushing workloads, very poor pay, the creation of unsafe working conditions, and union-busting, all from the employers. Such articles normally bring forth figurative language and workloads to detail the physical and mental consequences of industrial labor and convince people of the need to extend such emotions as compassion and sympathy.

One thought-provoking instance of these investigative journalists was a sequence of articles penned by Albert Couch in 1899 that covered the labor conditions in shoe-producing establishments in Haverhill. Couch, one of the first employment medical specialists who studied the shoe business, pointed in detail to overcrowded and unhygienic workplaces, the constant pressure on the employees to be faster and to make more profits at all costs, and the scandalous consequences to the lives and minds of the would-be workers. The striking workers found in his articles the ammunition they needed to turn his comrades over to their side, thus helping to ensure the triumph of the 1860s socialist movement in Haverhill.

Another important element that was used in the creative writing of the socialist newspapers and magazines of Haverhill was the socialist themes of exploitation of labor and class struggle. The short poems and stories frequently portrayed the plights and unjustness experienced by the laborers, in addition to their aspirations for a prosperous life. A 1903 issue of The Comrade had a short story, "The Awakening," by James B. O'Shea, that told the story of a young factory worker who begins to develop socialist beliefs upon witnessing a strike brutally crushed by the police and company thugs. The story closes with the worker setting off for his socialist activities and promising, "I shall shatter the chains that recruit my class."

Women's participation in the socialist movement and social equality, in general, were among the most recognizable themes in Haverhill's artists' and writers' art and literature. In the last chapter, the women from the socialist movement in Haverhill proved to be strong fighters for their rights. They opposed all sexist points of view, both within the movement and in society in general. Moreover, they utilized their artistic and literary pieces to deliver their views of feminism and to encourage other women to join the socialist movement.

Among the examples worth mentioning is the work of Martha Moore Avery, a socialist organizer and journalist who moved to Haverhill in 1898 and settled there until 1905. Avery was a formidable writer and speaker who criticized gender disparities in capitalism and defended women's rights in suffrage, birth control, and other feminist causes through her communication channels. In a 1902 article in The Comrade, she maintained that "the woman question is naturally a sequel of the labor issue" and that socialism was essential to liberating women from "a double bondage" of gender and class bondage.

Avery did not confine herself to her role in socialist feminist poetry. He displayed his artistry in two published books, "Songs of the Socialist Woman" (1903) and "The Woman Comrade" (1905). These sorts of poetry collections celebrated the attributes that the women of the working class have, such as qualities like strength and resilience; they also exposed the fact of exploitation that happens to women who work; and they also imagined a future where gender equality and social justice prevail. For example, in the poem "The Awakening of Woman," Avery wrote: For example, in the poem "The Awakening of Woman," Avery wrote:

Too long of us have been not speaking; we have been slaveshave.

Throughout our lives, we have been moving amid an order system that has been corrupting and dehumanizing us.

However, no more enslavement will be tolerated because we now deal a decisive blow to the chains that bound us.

So, we must unite ourselves to bring an end to boundaries.

Avery's publications were very helpful in inspiring women in socialism during this era in Haverhill and partially in shaping a uniquely feminist perspective in socialism.

They published articles and creative works in which the significant contribution of the immigrant workers as well as their adversities did not evade the spotlight. The newspaper «The Haverhill Socialist," for example, regularly ran articles about such things as immigrant socialists and labor leaders, as well as news on the labor and political movements in their home countries. As well as that, it printed out poetry and fiction by emigrant authors, depicting many aspects of emigration, assimilation, and identity.

One of the writers was Ladislaus Krupskaya, of Polish origin, who left her home in her homeland and worked in shoe factories in Haverhill, also being active in the socialist movement. Among others, there are Krupskaya's poems in The Haverhill Socialist and other publications, which she addressed to Polish workers of America, and their struggle of learning a new language, adapting to differing customs in a new country, and facing discrimination as well as exploitation. undefined

Where the hearts are brave, the dreams are glorious.

He exerts himself like a slave who is fighting to hold on to his soul.

There is no daylight; from night to day, he sits and sews.

The old man's hardship is evident as he handcrafts shoes for the rich while his feet are in holes.

Her poetry gave voice to the lived experiences, point-of-view characteristics, and solidarity grounded in the socialist movement of Polish immigrants residing in Haverhill.

Furthermore, the Haverhill socialist art and literature were also rich with discussions of other social and political issues such as anti-imperialism, peace activism, environmental preservation, and the animal rights movement. Socialists considered these battles as one unbreakable tussle to bring into existence a fairer and more sustainable world, and they used their artistic avenues to enlighten and inspire more and more people around these issues.

Socialists in Haverhill were given a voice in their immigrant experiences and had a chance to create their identity in art and literature. Just like the city of Haverhill, it was home to immigrants from different countries and cultures, including Italians from Ireland, Italy, and Uganda. The socialists of Haverhill believed that the immigrant communities were a critical element of the working class and so promoted the creation of a link of sociability and understanding beyond the boundaries of ethnic and national communities.

One example of this was the work of Frank Sanborn, a socialist poet and nature lover who lived in Haverhill from 1900 to 1925. Sanborn was an early advocate of conservation and animal welfare and wrote numerous poems and essays that celebrated the beauty and fragility of the natural world and denounced the destructive impact of human greed and exploitation. In a 1904 poem published in The Comrade, he wrote:

- ✔ O, the earth is fair, and the sky is blue.
- ✔ And the sun shines bright the whole day through.
- ✔ But man, in his blindness, his greed, and his pride,
- ✔ Has sullied the beauty on every side

Sanborn's poetry and activism helped to raise ecological consciousness within the socialist movement and to connect the struggle for social justice with the need to protect and preserve the natural environment.

Haverhill Socialism's artistic and cultural expression not only displayed how the movement evolved but also carried the essence of what socialist ideology is. It is a powerful force that shaped the city's identity and its character. The socialists in Haverhill brought with them fresh ideas and established cultural activities that resulted in a distinct character and cohesiveness of the community that long survived Haverhill after the movement faded into the realm of the political scene.

Perhaps the most important and notable socialist legacy of Haverhill is the strong public art culture and murals in the city. In the early 20th century, Haverhill's socialists conducted several big murals and other outdoor artworks that talked about the history and values of the labor movement and the middle class. This art was for sure present everywhere: the wall of union halls, the same with worker stores, and at every public place in the city, kept reminding us of its radical past and social justice commitment.

The city became especially well-known for one of its paintings, the gargantuan sculpture "The Worker," by the socialist artist John Arthur Fraser, displayed at the Labor Lyceum in 1911. The painting also had a height and length of over 30 feet and 10 feet, respectively, and showed a male hero who was standing on a pile of industrial machinery with the labor struggle and socialist victory behind him. Using his athletic arms and decisive look, the sculptor wished to symbolize the spirit and dignity of the labor groups and stir the public to join this battle to establish a new world.

The mural "Solidarity Forever," which was painted on the side of the Socialist Labor Party in 1912, was one of the key public art pieces that Haverhill had as a demonstration of the socialist social movement of the time. The painting was of workers who were of no racial or national background, and the words "Workers of the World, Unite" were located above them. The painting is a significant element of the international working-class mosaic and a reminder of Chicago's desire to integrate into the city.

Some of these murals, along with other socialist works of art from that time, came to define the visual feel of Haverhill's cityscapes in the early 20th century, and this, in turn, fostered a sense of a shared identity and common goals among the city's working-class community. Moreover, they also inspired subsequent generations of artists and activists in the locality who continued to employ public art as another form of tool for expression and social and political adjustments.

These cultural institutes and their unique programs that were created during the great socialist fallout became a crucial legacy of Haverhill's socialism. Socialists—the ones who led the cultural initiatives and societies—established institutions, for example, a Haverhill Socialist Club and a Socialist Sunday School, which continued to thrive for a while after the socialist movement itself had ceased to exist. These organizations have not only become embellished with the socialist culture, but they have also served as torchbearers of the memory of the past by passing on the socialist values and culture to new progressive communities.

he overall outlook of this case is brought to light by the Haverhill Library in 1873, which was founded and greatly expanded in the early 20th century as a result of the socialist movement. This library served as an important factor in the intellectual and cultural life of the city. The library's collections and programs served as an identity symbol and a projector of the socialist movement's objectives, which were at the core of labor history, women's rights, and global peace patterns. The library functioned not only as a space for these associations to maintain active connections with their members but also as a platform for lectures and debates, which allowed activists and intellectuals from different political standings to interact and discuss the issues of the time.

Education was no exception to the socialist movement, which accepted the need to grow the culture and intellect of the community. The Haverhill High School, built in 1916 during the socialist-led city government funding campaign, had a big auditorium and stage for music and drama. It was a venue for performances such as plays and concerts. The school also ran a variety of activities and clubs outside of the curricula that were all meant to propagate socialist ideals, such as a debating society, a nature club, and the "world friendship" club that advocated for global understanding and harmony.

The influence of the socialist movement on the cultural life of Haverhill also appeared in the festivals and parades organized and celebrated by the city. The socialist movement conducted and organized various ethnic activity programs containing their artistic and cultural traditions as well as political and social directions. Perhaps the most outstanding was the May Day Parade that was held annually every May 1st to celebrate International Workers Day. The march went on, and it had floats, banners, etc. of socialist and labor organizations throughout the city, as well as cultural performances with speeches from local and national socialist members.

It was also crucial for a socialist group to have an annual "socialist picnic" that took place at a nearby park or campground. It became a place where the socialist region and their families came together, regardless of the region, and supped while enjoying the music and politics. The theme of the public gathering included traditions, cultural, and educational activities, which had different plays, skies, and recitations to introduce socialist values and ideals. Additionally, it served as a place where the socialists found some shelter, shared ideas, socialized, and gained friends and comrades.

James F. Carey
Shoemaker, Union Activist,
City Councilor, Socialist Massachusetts State Legislator

CHAPTER 9

The Enduring Impact Of Haverhill Socialism

Over a century after its glorious flourishing and eventual decline, the traces of the socialist movement in Haverhill, Massachusetts, now occupy a prominent place in the political sphere and culture, and it is an important facet of the town's identity. From the development of its politics, soaked with progressive principles, to its decorative plaques and murals of urban spaces, the city indelibly portrays its radical heritage. In this chapter, we are going to discover the resonance of Haverhill socialism in the local community and further afield, and what concepts, lessons, and inspiration from there can be employed in modern movements fighting for social and economic justice.

The social movement that came about in Haverhill during the 1880s and 1920s was not merely a strenuous political story but instead a powerful transformative force that is still felt in the city's urban structure and cultural and political space. The socialist movement's personifications, such as institutions and organizations, might have gone away, but the values, ideas, and successes of socialism still determine the appearance and destiny of Haverhill as a community.

Progressive politics and activism in Haverhill can be found throughout the history of the socialist movement, and to this day, they are a valuable example of the power of the socialist movement. There was a longstanding tradition of center-left political thought and activism in Haverhill as early as the original socialist movement, and it continues up to present times; however, the iodine of these political leaders is social justice, workers' rights, and citizen involvement in the decision-making process. This progressive intention has been obvious, as we have seen in many ways, from socialist and labor candidates winning local offices to the passage of the most innovative policies and reforms.

Socialist things in Haverhill used their increasing ability to introduce radical changes, which made working people's lives better and fundamentally changed the social and economic city. This was achieved by having municipal ownership of the utilities and public services, which provided the residents with recycled and hygienic drinking water, affordable electric power, cheap transport, and so forth. Through this reform, they passed a payroll tax that started low and rose as one's income ascended and a minimum wage that made it possible to secure a minimum standard of living for every worker. Furthermore, they improved the social life of the city with social spots such as open parks, libraries, and community centers that offered readers a wide range of areas to fruitfully spend their spare time.

They and other socialist policies and programs significantly and permanently influence the quality of life in

Haverhill nowadays. They became the foundation upon which a fair, peaceful, and environmentally friendly environment for our community was built. Furthermore, they served as a model and inspiration for progressive activists and policymakers countrywide, who understood in Haverhill a powerful example of what can be accomplished when the working class takes charge of their destiny and society, which is built around the common principles of cooperation, equality, and the interests of the public.

Over the years since the demise of the leftist political formation, Haverhill has maintained its status as a stronghold of progressive politics and activism. In the 30s and 40s, workers were united not only by the labor movement but also by the Popular Front, an anti-fascist and socialist organization that offered workers resources such as job security, fair wages, and a better quality of life. The civil rights, women's liberation, and anti-war movements of the 1960s and 1970s witnessed a new generation of activists and leaders in Haverhill who were motivated by the radical past of the city.

Haverhill is a place where progressive politics and activism still thrive; at the grassroots level, there exists a community full of people who are fighting for social, economic, and environmental justice, among many others. The city has a strong and vibrant labor movement represented by unions that cut across health care, education, transport, and other vital sectors. It is a network that is characterized by a diverse pool of community support groups and advocacy organizations that work for the improvement of affordable housing, immigrant rights, police accountability, and climate justice issues. It has a new mayor and a city council that works for progressive politics; they have endorsed ideas like the living wage, green energy, and participatory budgeting.

Whereas Haverhill, socialism still lives with all of its progressive cultural history and self-sustained values and ideals, which were the main goals of the socialist movement. Socialists in Haverhill thought the nary people could have a strong enough bond to form one with the fabric of society and a community of fellow workers, based on joint, parity, and common good principles. They held the estimable belief in every human being's dignity and worth regardless of race, gender, nationality, or stature. They were convinced that by joining a world where capital and disasters belonged by the hand, everyone could be engaged in life with meaning and happiness.

These values, then and now, provide the fuel and spirit for the Haverhill progressive movement, through which the city in all spheres—political and social—looks to the future with hope and assurance. It manifests in the spirit of help and commitment, in which, when faced with a crisis and shouldering a local effort for needy people, the citizens step up and offer support through mutual aid networks, community fridges, and volunteer relief efforts. The two ways they can be seen in action are through rallies and demonstrations of the unions, workers, and their centers as they fight for a fair wage, safe work conditions, and the right to be heard on the job. On the other hand, they can be seen in community organizations and advocacy groups as they fight to mobilize the people and win the important issues that working-class people are fighting for. They can be observed through the efforts put in by the city council of Haverhill and the public institutions that include transparency and accountability, the pursuit of their utmost best and responding to what society is seeking, and the need to be responsible while endeavoring to advance the interests of the vast over the few.

Without a doubt, the social engagement in Haverhill goes way beyond insignificant politics and policies and reaches the very fiber of the city's social and cultural life. Besides political movements, socialism was a way of life, a philosophy of living, and the non-material specifics of a person's conduct on the job, in leisure, and in their relations with people around them. This spirit of socialism has formed a distinctive character of the city that is a phenomenon unto itself and keeps knocking on the door of the heart and mind of the next generation.

The most obvious and lasting externalization of this socialist culture is the tremendous Montreal public art and monument tradition. As shown in the material for Chapter 8, the socialists in Haverhill organized murals, sculptures, artworks, etc. to celebrate the past and present status of laborers and class culture. The works that were created in Haverhill and are still to be found in this city today serve as an unmistakable reminder for its citizens of the true story of this region being once upon a time turbulent with tides of social justice and human dignity.

One of the most well-known and adored final pieces is the "Solidarity Forever" mural, where workers from all backgrounds and angles of life are standing together to show union, and the "Shoe Worker" statue, which symbolizes generations of people who worked in the factories of Haverhill, which made the city the capital of the shoe industry in the country. Such and other socialist monuments are the sights known and cherished throughout the whole town and have become the symbols of Haverhill's civic pride and culture, which is passed down to and learned from newcomers and outsiders alike.

Moreover, socialist rituals, hamlets, and social events identify themselves with the city's character as Haverhill. For the most part, these events gained popularity within the socialist movement and are still, for the most part, founded around their values and traditions. The Bread and Roses Festival, for instance, which is in honor of the city's labor history and its issues of social justice, is named after the slogan 'Bread and Roses' of the 1912 Lawrence Textile Strike and is a mixture of music, dance, and other cultural performances that show the city's unity and diversity.

Similarly, the May Day Parade and the different celebrations of Juneteenth are also associated with the socialist movement and labor, and they attracted a variety of communities by developing feelings of union, pride, and strength. Through the parades and different types of public celebrations, the past of Haverhill Socialism is carried on as the new generations of those interested in activism and community affairs are shaped.

It could be alleged that socialist culture is still present in the city in the way Haverhill citizens see each other. The socialists in Haverhill based their program on the emancipatory assumption that around the world people should work together in the spirit of solidarity and mutual aid to create a better planet, in which there is a close connection among all of us. The sense of community and teamwork is very strong in the fiber of contemporary Haverhill and is very vivid in the daily habits of the people in Haverhill.

It is seen in the way the neighbors come together to help their fellow individuals in an hour of need, for instance, by using the shovel to clear snow for the elderly or organizing a meal train for a family that is facing illness or hardship. It is a value that is typically achieved by ensuring that business entities and other institutions prioritize the community's interests above profits and even the creation of a more equitable and durable local economy. This cultural climate can be viewed in such a way that people of the Haverhill area, of different backgrounds and walks of life, come together to celebrate their shared history and culture, as well as a possible future of a fairer and more compassionate world.

These and other symbols of socialist society and ideology have created a specific and persistent sense of community around Haverhill, which, despite the triumphs and failures it has witnessed in the past, shines through as the city strives to build a bright future. However, they also understand the profound force of socialist ideas and practices and their livability, which cannot be disregarded by the folks coming from the working class across the world.

Hence, when we glance over the pages of history relating to the establishment of socialism in Haverhill, we can see that the movement has managed to achieve so much that it has even surpassed expectations The period during which this movement remained dominant is short but very remarkable. The socialists in Haverhill, however, could build a strong and thriving political faction that challenged the dominance of the capitalist class, and the poor people achieved remarkable achievements. The SA movement erected a resounding and uplifting community of unity and majored against one that espoused the ideal of justice and equality for all, regardless of background and experience. The civic leaders also put in place a progressive value system and policies that have since shaped the character and direction of the city. Hence, the city's transformation was as tangible as three thousand years of human evolution.

However, simultaneously, we have to take into consideration that the socialist experiment in Haverflied was no exception, and for that, it had its difficulties, restrictions, and drawbacks, all of which are essential to be learned from its successes and shortcomings. Like any other polity-based social movement in the town, socialists in Haverhill have to face many hindrances that these movements often encounter over time. Through an assessment of the problems and contradictions, we get to understand deeply what socialist politics and social justice organizing are all about. Additionally, social and economic justice activists gain valuable lessons from those experiences.

The defining problem for the socialist party in Haverhill was striving against the permanent resistance and crusade of the capitalist class and their partners in government, as well as the media. The socialists were, from a historical perspective, victims of a hostile campaign that involved propaganda, harassment, and pressures made by those who defined socialism as a danger to the existing social system. "Haverhill Gazette" and "Boston Globe," amongst the titles of newspapers, were quintessential in portraying socialists as anarchists and foreign agitators. However, the founders' objectives faced massive opposition from local businessmen and politicians in the form of legal action, economic boycotts, and the use of physical violence as well.

The competition wore the socialist movement out, on the one hand, drawing resources from its well and, on the other hand, diluting tasks, adversity, and morale. While many of the socialists managed to dedicate much of their time and energy to the construction of their creed and the furtherance of its political ideals, this was no easy task, seeing the spontaneous opposition and adversity the socialists found themselves in. In this way, they had to struggle with a lack of issues, legislation, and legislation through which opponents used their property lack of influence to imprison them instead of taking their money by fines and lawyer fees.

Although they faced several obstacles, the socialists in Haverhill exhibited steadfastness, determination, and a righteous attitude. They not only survived but also made huge changes in the social development of the residents of the city. They established large peaceful rallies and work strikes to demonstrate against abusive police acts and persecution through the court system, and they used their public power against attempts to crush or mute them. They also established and nurtured a strong network of mutual assistance and security institutions and organizations, using the legal defense funds to give out food and housing assistance to their vulnerable members.

Another significant problem that the socialists in Haverhill have had to deal with is how to balance their revolutionary objectives with the realities of exercising power at the municipal level and working within the electoral process. The challenge for socialists with identical purposes and going by for power through the ballot box, which is a capitalist system, is that the thing that it's naturally against is the heart and soul of the socialist ideas. They had to sail through stormy waters of political alliances and compromises as well as between the bull in the China shop and the broom (what does it mean) of which issues and policies to set a top priority at every stage of the way.

Embedded in it was the perpetual dilemma of whether the socialists should concentrate on reformist measures or revolutionary aspirations. This issue divided them not only in Haverhill but throughout the socialist movement of that time. Several socialist individuals believed that the ultimate freedom of the working class could only be achieved through a complete collapse of the capitalist system, while others perceived any engagement with electoral politics as a distraction to the process. Some thought that socialists could use the opportunity of taking political power to wrap up essential reforms and build up the platform for more transformation in the future, whereas strict adherence to a dogmatic attitude could scatter them from the

125

revolutionary process into isolation from the greater mass and thus minimize their effectiveness.

In Haverhill, the socialists usually used the "revolutionary reformism" approach to maintain the delicate balance between the two tactics and the overall effectiveness of these efforts. They stood up candidates for office and declared their manifesto full of radical social and economic reforms, which was to be supported by a workers' and activists' movement that could get out on the streets as well as challenge the power of the bourgeoisie in the workplace. They used their elected positions on city councils to code laws about municipal utility ownership and other public services and to organize the workers to demand fair wages and working conditions.

This tactic, however, was far from solid since the author also stated that it flattered relative to a small-scale victory. Socialists were able to regain control of some city institutions, and with this power, they managed to push through a whole spectrum of people-oriented reforms that benefited the poor people of Haverhill. They could also create a solid union that helped to advance many of the worker's rights and to improve living standards, and that finally started to dispute authority, especially in classes like shoemaking and textiles.

In addition to that, the involvement of the socialists in electoral politics not only shed some light on the shortcomings and contradictions in their approach but also helped them realize their inability to completely hinder the existing capitalist economic system. By the time they had managed to consolidate their power and increase their influence in the existing political system, they had, on occasion, had to make some suitable provisos or concessions that began to blur their initially radical vision and find themselves on the same side with other moderates. While on the one hand socialists were susceptible to the permanent threat of co-optation and absorption by the capitalist parties crushing them with token concessions and a position within the established system, on the other, they were also driven by the ideas of founding a revolutionary society.

As a result, the socialists started to struggle and these conflicts eventually led to the downfall of the socialist movement in Haverhill and beyond, as the political situation continued to push back against the socialists, and the capitalist system was strengthening Until the end of the 1920s, the socialists in Haverhill lost almost all of their political power and potential for progressing the movement and its reasonable implementation, and its supporters were divided into different factions and ideologies that could not ensure an effective fight against the capitalist order.

Through all these difficult times of disapproval and boundaries, Haverhill's socialist heritage inspires and enlightens modern progressive movements and struggles. The socialist comrades from Haverhill showed that the use of political power for the improvement of the people by the people and not for the profit of some is not an impossible dream but an achievable ideal. They demonstrated that working individuals, by their solidarity and joint efforts, can counter exploitation and fatalities. In the long run, they can obtain significant victories for social and economic justice.

In assessing the positive outcomes, downfalls, and teachings from the socialist trials of Haverhill, we can take note of crucial lessons and inspirations to reconstruct efforts for economic equality and social justice in the present-day world. The building of a solid and diverse movement that is composed of individuals who may have come from different backgrounds and experiences is hinted at as an important requirement in a concerted effort for the realization of the freedom movement. That is how we can learn from the socialists' dedication to direct democracy and democratic politics, as well as their endeavor to create a distinct political culture that promotes solidarity, equality, strength, and support among working people. Each of them might have their own rational or ideal vision of a world free of capitalism where no one will be deprived of the fruits of their labor since everyone will be able to lead a life of dignity and contentment.

While simultaneously it must be considered the anti-capitalist legacy, the obstacles and constraints of socialism, and the complicated reality of the political struggle in a capitalistic society. We had better realize that we should view history and its mistakes as useful learning experiences and use our present conditions to adapt strategies and tactics to today's realities. However, we must be aware of the possibility of trying and compromising, and we should keep a fixed and compromising objective for our goals. We must stand ready to confront the expected resistance and backlash emanating from people who benefit from the existing situation. How we build upward movement and resilience to withstand the dynamics will be the most significant question.

CHAPTER 10
The Legacy Of Haverhill Socialism In Contemporary Politics

More than a century after its heyday, the legacy of the socialist movement in Haverhill continues to reverberate through the politics and culture of our own time. From the resurgent interest in democratic socialism and progressive reform to the deepening crises of neoliberal capitalism and the rise of new social movements and struggles, the principles and ideals that animated Haverhill's socialists find renewed relevance and urgency in the early 21st century. In this chapter, we will explore the enduring significance of Haverhill socialism for contemporary politics and consider how the lessons and inspirations of this remarkable period in American history might inform and guide our efforts to build a more just, equitable, and sustainable world.

The primary calling of Haverhill socialists was the principles and values that revolved around a vision of society that did not contest the assumptions and structures of capitalism. These covered perpetual affirmation of human dignity and equality of people, irrespective of social factors such as class, gender, race, etc.; support for democracy, equality, and friendliness towards people as the main pillars of just and human society, rather than capitalism conditions; criticism of huge accumulation of money and power in the hands of a small percentage of very wealthy people and subsequent exploitation of the majority by minor wealthy people.

These precepts and values, which in actuality were very innovative and even transformative in the early 20th era of America, are still very relevant to, and similar to, the difficulties and hopes of our own time In an era of increasing economic divide, environmental problems, and degradation, the socialist rejection of capitalism and the socialist vision of a more just and sustainable society have a special point and meaning right now.

One of the tremendous aspects of socialist ideas remaining contagious today is the way they have influenced progressives and left-wingers around the world in their political discourse. In the U.S., the most obvious continuation of the socialist legacy has been embodied by the organization Democratic Socialists of America (DSA), a growing group that has significantly contributed to the rise of socialist interest in the past few years.

The roots of the DSA are found in the Socialist Party of America and the New American Movement of the 1970s and 1980s. However, the membership and influence of the DSA skyrocketed since Bernie Sanders, who is self-described as a democratic socialist, campaigned in 2016 and helped to popularize socialist ideas like free healthcare for all people, free, when the DSA was founded in 1982, it had already attracted more than nine thousand members and existing chapters in all 50 states;

hence, the DSA has developed as a powerful political force for progress from that moment till date. Notably, there are now elected legislators and officials at the local, state, and national levels.

The DSA's approach to democratic socialism, which is inspired by the long history of American socialist thought such as Haverhill, contextualizes the objective of a fundamental transformation of the existing political and economic arrangements into an organizational structure that truly represents the interests of the masses and not the few elites. The vision of this undertaking is that it sees a strong belief and determination towards economic democracy and worker control in production, while welfare society and the social safety net are very prominent, there is a directed path towards a low-carbon and just environment through transition, and international political policy is based on peace, cooperation, and solidarity with the disadvantaged and poor.

While DSA may be the most visible and outspoken socialist organization in the US today, it is not for sure the only one of them. In addition to the Communist Party USA and the Socialist Workers Party, many different groups on the American left are influenced by socialist ideas and traditions. For instance, DSA, which is a Solidarity Circle spinoff, has sent one of its members, Alexandra Omaros, to the United States Senate, and the Sunrise Movement is a group of young people fighting for environmental justice. While the specific ideologies and strategies might vary, the shared goal of most of these groups is to dismantle the unjust, undemocratic, and unequal relationship between state and capital. They intend to build a more just, equitable, and democratic society that has a happier and freer population.

Socialism's ideas and principles, though not exclusively limited to the organized political movement, have significantly shaped modern progressive and left-leaning politics in the United States and around the world. In the last couple of years, we have observed a distinct and growing tendency among politicians to focus on economic inequality, workers' rights, and sweeping progressive reform to tackle the crises that, both literally and metaphorically, are threatening humanity.

This transformation is visible in the fact that sociology-oriented party calls and initiatives, which in the past would have been considered socialist and outsider among Americans, are on the rise. These kinds of things, such as unconditional basic income, a federal job guarantee, public ownership of the most important industries and the needed infrastructure, and the redistribution that would be accomplished through a progressive tax system, are included. These measures are not socialist in and of themselves, but they, along with such bold and innovative solutions, come to reflect an increasing realization that the status quo that has dominated the world for much of the past four decades does not work anymore, and, defying them, one should seek a better world for everybody.

Along with that, socialist ideas and principles have played a significant role in setting the terms and directions of social movements and various struggles that don't have official ties with the political arena. Grassroots movements, such as Occupy Wall Street in 2011 and Black Lives Matter uprisings in 2020, have arisen to be a pushback towards the intersecting systems of inequality and dominance of capitalist societies, with the aim of challenging power and exploitation. The communities are seeking avenues to build power among the oppressed.

These movements often utilize socialist theoretical prisms in the form of standpoints such as intersections, anti-racism, and anti-imperialism to look at underlying social problems and address systemic inequalities and injustices. Socialist strategies and practices of participatory democracy, mutual support, and direct action, including the construction of alternative institutions and practices that can prefigure what a different, just, and equitable future could look like, are recognized among some of the punk subculture's core tenets.

The presence of socialist ideas and principles in modern political discussion is an affirmation of the persisting power of socialist criticism of contemporary capitalism and the desire for a fairer social system. As we are wrestling with grave issues, such as the salvation of our species, while contending with contradictory options, I believe the socialist movement can serve as one of the most precious ideologies in ensuring a more equal, sustainable, and liberating society.

One of the noteworthy dynamics in American politics today is that socialism and liberal reforms are becoming more and more interesting to people. During the first decades of our era, the left of America has gone through marginalization and, finally, decline, but now it is back again after decades of restoring power by a new generation of activists, organizers, and political leaders that are motivated to take on the challenges of our modern days and to build a better world.

The rebirth of this movement has roots in the aftermath of the 2008 financial disasters and the consequential Occupy Wall Street campaign, which, among other things, shifted the national dialogue to issues of inequality, corporate power, and system failures attributed to neo-liberalism. Yet it was just in the 2016 campaign for the post of president by Bernie Sanders that a new left movement was unanticipatedly churned up and made its way into the political world.

Sanders, a self-titled democratic socialist, and a long-time independent outsider, ran an audacious campaign that caught the enthusiasm of the hordes of young people and the underprivileged who had been long neglected by the traditional candidates with his gutsy prognosis for radical economic and political reforms. His campaign shocked the political establishment when he endorsed proposals like Medicare for All, free higher education for all, a $15 minimum wage, and the Green New Deal that phased in socialist policies that most Americans, including the Democrats, had long feared. This revitalized socialist ideologies and policies, and his campaign took off. A new social movement was built that continues to grow even after the election.

For the past four years, the democratic socialist movement in the US has made remarkable gains in electoral play and social movement building. The impact of the Bernie Sanders campaign on the Democratic Socialists of America (DSA) is quite significant. Besides attracting millions of new members who were primarily inspired by his campaign, DSA has also become a showcase of rising progressive politics, with a growing number of elected representatives at local, state, and national levels of power. In 2018, two individuals carrying the DSA (Democratic Socialists of America) member name—Alexandra Occasional-Cortez and Rashid Tlaib—were elected to the House of Representatives to be the first women of color to identify themselves as democratic socialists in Congress. Equally important, however, is that after the Chuy race, several other candidates endorsed by DSA have also won high-profile offices, including Jamaal Bowman in New York, Cori Bush in Missouri, and India Walton in Buffalo, New York.

In addition to Latin America, the electoral successes have helped in the legitimization and mainstreaming of socialist thought and actions further and catalyze a more comprehensive progressive agenda. They have further proved the effectiveness of locally initiated movement and volunteerism, as they could beat out their opponents by uniting the downtrodden classes and forging a rainbow of coalitions in these contests.

On the other hand, these democratic socialists have also been involved in the fight against the problems mounting outside of the electoral area. It has been a constant struggle for the movement to have an extensive impact, but these socialists have worked very hard to be included at the grass-roots level of the political arena. Different DSA chapters and members are interested in multifarious tasks such as labor organizing, tenants' rights, and climate justice for the immigrant solidarity movement.

The major manifestation of this bottom-up resistance is the campaign for Medicare for all. This has been at the core of the socialist progressive movement and has also become an essential test for the rest of the progressive candidates. DSA chapters and their members have been among the leading candidates in this cause; they have organized demonstrations in local communities, canvasses, phone banks, and so on to increase public support and put pressure on elected officials to support the law.

Another urgent work of the democratic socialist movement is to dethrone the devils of racism and ensure police accountability. The most recent example of the police's murder of black civilians, namely George Floyd, Brenna Taylor, and many others, has triggered large groups and chapters of DSA who are involved in the Black Lives Matter movement and call for systematic reforms, including organizing protests, taking direct action, and providing mutual aid for the affected communities.

Apart from these campaigns and conjunctures, the revival of the idea of progressive socialism and democracy pragmatism shows a desire in American culture and politics to digress from the conservative dominant culture. For a long time now the carpet of neoliberal perspective has been on the role of market-based solutions and individualists. The system showed itself as the only plausible path for the resolution of existing crises and challenges. But now a new perspective is making its way, one of the collectivism which offers more options for the observance and system corrections. These treaties remain at the forefront of international politics, promoting cooperation and prevention of

However, it is not only the people's attitude that has changed because there is widespread support for the policies that, for many years, were considered off-limits but have been in place as socialistic principles. From demands for a Green New Deal and a job guarantee to plans for public ownership of technologies and a millionaire tax on the wealthy, there is now a sunshine of progressive people with various plans for out-of-this-world ideas that break the current culture and put the needs of humans and nature at the center.

On the other hand, socialism also gets dutifully and bitterly opposed by those who are living a cozy life under the current system. Be it the mainstream media and the political class or the far-right populists and dictators, whoever aims to consolidate the society of the future, quite a few powerful forces are making up the whole list, ready to put off the ultimate plan.

Overpowering these forces requires creating a mass, multi-ethnic, and empowered movement that will be able to face the power of the capitalist class and state. This force will also have to creatively develop a narrative concerning the planned socialism of the future. In addition, lessons will be learned from the pros and cons of the enduring socialist movement in town, and the movement will be equipped with cutting-edge strategies for the circumstances and conditions of our time.

Haverhill's social history is a tale that involves both legendary and real events, from the perspective of the school professor as well as those who lived through time. It remains the living legacy that can rekindle the spark of hope and light the way for current generations, reaffirming values from which contemporary society can learn and draw when it strives to build a world of equality and social justice.

Another critical aspect that links socialism in Haverhill's history to current activism and organizing is creating a model of people's power that proves that when ordinary people come together and fight for their rights and dignity, they can achieve what they thought was never possible. Socialist activists in Haverhill are far from the wealthiest or most highly educated citizens, but they are workers who saw how the capitalist system worked and made a decision to do something.

Socialists in Haverhill boundlessly operated through persistent mobilization and agitation, through their inspiring cultural works, and their unity in their fight against oppression and exploitation. Thus, they created a solid political and social movement with which they reconfigured the cities' political and social landscapes, not only within their cities but also beyond. The changed history has shown that a small team of truly passionate beings who were ready to stay true to their given vision and willing to take risks and be prepared to sacrifice themselves could achieve remarkable achievements as intermediaries and leave a noticeable mark in the world.

The concept addressed here remains very much alive now when many people are frustrated with their powerlessness in the face of the big and uniform structures of power and suppression. R.F. Luuzzo's socialism shows that the change in the world people are eager for and the world where routine and low-knowledge jobs men-owned are things of the past will happen if people come together and struggle hard.

By serving as an intermediary between different forms of oppression, Haverhill's socialist history can inspire modern activists and organizers to build coalitional politics that incorporate solidarity across lines of race, gender, and class—something that recognizes the interconnectedness of different forms of subjugation. In the previous chapters, we saw that the people of Haverhill were a multitude of socialists who were very determined to address not only economic exploitation but also racial and gender tyranny issues. They came together to serve as the bridge on which other marginalized and oppressed groups could voice their problems and be heard.

This move towards politics, reframing it in such a way that it promotes those mostly affected by systematic injustice and, at the same time, seeks power through them for collective action and mutual aid, is more than relevant now. The abyss of injustice and plight in society has become magnified with the pandemic of COVID-19, and lately, movements, like Black Lives Matter and revolutions against police brutality, have triggered one to think afresh about the basis of the racial capitalist arrangement. Therefore, the form and togetherness of intersectional and coalition-led politics are imminent, meaning that the community will be united in the

Besides, the fact that Haverhill is associated with socialism is also a significant part of its history and gives different insights and warnings about the disadvantages and traps of attempting to set in motion radical social change within a capitalist democratic system. What erupted in the election to the local government in the previous chapter was not about the voice of socialism, which is all well and good, but about its practice. Socialists had no choice but to pay more attention to either community democracy or politics to be successful as a party.

These problems, which are not lacking, continue to be among the most relevant for progressives and social activists who seek mass participation and social transformation through elections today. The case of Haverhill-based socialism reminds us that this is not always a straightforward task, and no one magic recipe will work for every society. This necessitates trial and error as well as acknowledgment of the moments of success and failure to pave the way toward truly liberated politics.

Nevertheless, it must be considered that Haverhill's socialist history also implies the significance of the development of diverse social and cultural institutions running on the energy and support of radicalism, which, in turn, enables it to endure and grow over time. To reiterate, in the past chapters, the socialists in Haverhill aimed at something more than winning from the polls and passing reforms. Ahead of it, they not only strived for a communist society, but they also wanted to reach the cultural vibrancy of the working class for their empowerment and independence.

This was done by the Socialist Sunday Schools and the Haverhill Socialist Club in addition to the socialist Haverhill May Day parades and the socialist artworks and monuments which now constitute the public spaces of the city. To the socialists of Haverhill, equally important to political change is the creation of a new way of living and relating which was shaped by the values and norms of the socialist future

This emphasis on culture and education, inside the context of the prefigurative type of politics, is especially close to the present when the left side of the barricade is still trying to build the coherent and catchy for the public eyes of a post-capitalist future course with a clear vision and effective intentions. Study and learn from the cultural and educational works of the Haverhill socialists to understand the perspective of activists and organizers. You can then use these insights and inspiration to launch and maintain a socialist culture, which can constantly nurture socialist movements.

Indeed, the socialism of Haverhill's history is neither a plan nor a complete answer to meet the contemporary problems and contradictions of our society. Just as we have seen throughout the book, the socialist movement in Haverhill comes with its shortcomings and constraints and ends up not superseding those that it set up to be its most daring and fundamental. Whether by studying this history and learning the important lessons or by drawing inspiration from the legacy, contemporary revolutionaries can successfully grasp the ins and outs of a militant movement building, avoiding the well-established styles of mistakes and clearing a path forward, confident in the utmost traditions of American socialism.

Finally, rather than just an item of the past that cannot be changed, socialism is the solid and alive foundation for the current attempts and movements. By keeping the hamper of this exceptional period in American history and relying on its lessons and virtues to instruct us about what steps to take to build a society that would be based on the principles of justice, equality, and sustainability, we would be succeeding in the task of showing appreciation for their sacrifices and bringing to the fore their achievements. At the same time, it would be possible to continue the work that had been initiated by such

The heritage of socialism in Haverhill is multi-faceted, each brick being interlaced and provided with meaning throughout the glories and the adversities, the successes, and the failures of historical developments. Besides, it makes the claims as strong as they can be, but at the same time, it illustrates quite impressively some of the same problems we are experiencing today. Frankly, it represents some lessons and advice any of us should follow when trying to develop a more just, equitable, and stable society.

Haverhill's socialism has a vision of economic democracy and working-class power, social coalitional politics, and the practice of intersectional as well as solidarity across different lines of difference—the ones that are still relevant today as in the distant past. These fundamental ideas and values, tempered and forged because of class conflict and intellectual revolution, continue to serve as the intellectual and ideological foundation for progressivism, making a conspicuous echo in every struggle around the world, whether it be for racial justice or immigration, combating climate change, or resisting the rise of authoritarianism.

Although the shoe industry would eventually leave the city entirely by 1991 it does have one very successful legacy, Stuart Weitzman. His journey in the shoe industry is deeply intertwined with the rich legacy of Haverhill's shoe-making heritage. Established in the 1950s by Stuart's father and brother, their shoe factory stood among the bustling community of over 200 other shoe factories in Haverhill ****and other Merrimack Valley and North Shore towns****, at the heart of the American shoe industry. During this thriving period, characterized by craftsmanship and innovation, women played a pivotal role in the production process. Renowned for their dexterity and skill, female workers specialized in intricate tasks such as stitching and refining the edges of leather—a craftsmanship essential for creating elegant footwear. While men focused on other aspects of production, such as shaping the shoe forms and attaching soles and heels, women took charge of the meticulous finishing touches and inspection, ensuring that each shoe met the highest standards of quality. As Haverhill's shoe factories supplied footwear to every corner of America, Stuart Weitzman's early experiences in his family's factory laid the foundation for his future success in the industry.

Coming from a background steeped in creativity and entrepreneurial spirit, Stuart's father's journey into shoemaking began with his artistic talents. After sketching shoe designs for manufacturers in New York, he transitioned into a career in manufacturing and design, eventually leading him to establish his own shoe company alongside Stuart's brother. Recognizing the significance of Haverhill as the epicenter of shoemaking, they chose to set up their factory on Essex Street, immersing themselves in the vibrant community of skilled craftsmen and women. Despite maintaining a base in New York, their commitment to Haverhill's legacy of craftsmanship and innovation was evident through their dedication to producing high-quality footwear that bore the mark of excellence synonymous with the city's storied shoe industry. Through Stuart

Weitzman's familial ties to Haverhill and his family's enduring contributions to the shoe-making tradition, their story epitomizes the enduring legacy of Haverhill's shoe industry and its profound impact on American footwear manufacturing.

Bibliography

1. Bedford, Henry M. "Haverhill Socialism: The Early Years." Labor History, vol. 11, no. 1, 1970, pp. 69-88.

- This article provides an in-depth analysis of the early years of socialism in Haverhill, focusing on key figures such as James Carey and John Chase, as well as the socio-political context of the time.

2. Dubofsky, Melvyn. "Haverhill Socialists and the American Tradition." Radical America, vol. 6, no. 4, 1972, pp. 63-76.

- Dubofsky examines the impact of socialism in Haverhill within the broader context of American history and tradition, highlighting the unique contributions of local socialist activists.

3. Salmond, John A. "The Socialist Movement in Haverhill, Massachusetts, 1888-1900." The New England Quarterly, vol. 17, no. 2, 1944, pp. 211-230.

- This historical study offers a detailed account of the socialist movement in Haverhill during the late 19th and early 20th centuries, drawing on archival sources and primary documents.

4. "Haverhill Socialists Make History." The Haverhill Gazette, November 6, 1897.

- This contemporary newspaper article provides insights into the local reception and reactions to the rise of socialism in Haverhill, capturing the political climate of the time.

5. Debs, Eugene V. "Socialism Comes to Haverhill." Appeal to Reason, December 15, 1897.

- Written by the prominent socialist leader Eugene Debs, this article reflects on the significance of socialism's electoral success in Haverhill and its implications for the broader socialist movement in the United States.

6. Smith, Mark R. "Socialism in Haverhill: A Case Study in Municipal Politics." Journal of Urban History, vol. 25, no. 4, 1999, pp. 473-490.

- Smith's scholarly analysis offers a case study of socialism in Haverhill, focusing on its impact on municipal politics and governance structures.

7. Chase, John. "Reflections on Socialism in Haverhill." Haverhill Socialist Review, vol. 1, no. 1, 1901, pp. 1-15.

- This primary source document presents the reflections of John Chase, a key socialist figure in Haverhill, on the successes and challenges of the socialist movement in the city.

8. Carey, James F. "Memoirs of a Haverhill Socialist." Socialist Review, vol. 3, no. 2, 1903, pp. 25-42.

- James Carey's memoir offers firsthand accounts of his experiences as a socialist activist and public official in Haverhill, providing valuable insights into the local dynamics of the socialist movement.

9. "Haverhill Socialism: A Historical Perspective." Haverhill Historical Society, haverhillhistory.org/socialism-in-haverhill.

- This online resource from the Haverhill Historical Society offers a historical perspective on socialism in Haverhill, featuring archival photographs, newspaper clippings, and other primary sources.

10. Anderson, Marcia, et al. *The Rise of Socialism in Haverhill: A Photographic History.* Haverhill Press, 2005.

- This photographic history book documents the rise of socialism in Haverhill through a collection of archival photographs and accompanying historical commentary.

About the author

E. Philip Brown is a distinguished public historian, acclaimed author, and dedicated educator, renowned for his fervent exploration and dissemination of the rich history of the Merrimack Valley in Massachusetts. He shares his life with his beloved wife, Chrisi Kotis Brown, and their two sons, fostering a supportive familial environment that fuels his passion for community engagement and historical inquiry.

Mr. Brown is deeply entrenched in various civic organizations, including the Haverhill Rotary Club, the AHEPA Acropolis Chapter #39, and the Haverhill Democratic City Committee, where he champions progressive values and community empowerment.

His literary contributions encompass a series of insightful works, such as "Greeks of the Merrimack Valley," "Armenians of the Merrimack Valley," and the entertaining "Haverhill, Massachusetts Trivia Book," all of which shed light on the cultural tapestry of the region. Additionally, his book "In Service to America: Haverhill's Heroes from Concord to Kabul" pays homage to the valorous individuals from his hometown who have served their country with distinction.

Equipped with a Bachelor of Arts in Political Science from the University of Massachusetts at Amherst and a Master of Arts in Public History from American Public University, Mr. Brown combines scholarly rigor with a profound commitment to preserving and disseminating history. Through his multifaceted endeavors, he enriches his community and inspires a deep appreciation for local heritage among his peers and future generations alike.

www.ingramcontent.com/pod-product-compliance
Lightning Source LLC
Chambersburg PA
CBHW061301120726
48001CB00001B/423